The Wizard in the Tree

The Wizard in the Tree

by LLOYD ALEXANDER

Illustrated by Laszlo Kubinyi

A YEARLING BOOK

Published by
Dell Publishing Co., Inc.
1 Dag Hammarskjold Plaza
New York, New York 10017

Yearling ® TM 913705, Dell Publishing Co., Inc.

ISBN: 0–440–49556–3

Reprinted by arrangement with E. P. Dutton, a division of
Elsevier-Dutton Publishing Co., Inc.

Printed in the United States of America
First Yearling printing—March 1981

CW

For those who don't expect miracles,
but hope for them anyway.

CHAPTER 1

 Mallory's oak was down. It lay where the woodcutters felled it. The villagers hired to clear that stretch of woods had already moved on, leaving a wake of toppled trees and raw stumps. Once, Mallory had pretended the old oak was her enchanted tower that would stand forever; now it sprawled with limbs tangled in the underbrush. She would have turned bitterly away, but then she saw it: a gray wisp curling from the trunk. Falling, the tree had split along much of its length and something was caught there; likely a squirrel or weasel. She hurried through brambles that plucked at her skirt, set down her basket, knelt, and peered into the crack.

What she had taken for the tail of some small animal was, instead, the tip of a straggling beard. A sharp-pointed nose jutted from the splintered wood; two eyes glared up at her. From deep within the trunk came a tart voice:

"When you have quite finished staring, I suggest you make some effort to get me out of here."

Mallory's jaw dropped, she fell back on her heels, trembling too much to run and too curious to do so even if she had been able. What came suddenly to her mind was the old tale of the dwarf with his beard caught in a stump. This creature, however, had all of himself trapped and he was bigger than any dwarf she had imagined.

"Enough!" snapped the voice. "Get on with it. Now!"

Despite her bewilderment, Mallory sprang to obey. She braced herself and took a firm hold, bending the strength of her arms and hands to force open the crack. She desperately wished for a hatchet, an iron bar, even a knife; the woodcutters had left not so much as an ax handle behind them. She halted, breathless, shaking her torn fingers.

Her glance fell on a pointed stone. She snatched it up and worked it into the crevice. With a second stone, she pounded the makeshift wedge as far as it would go, then looked for another.

The tree, meantime, had begun rocking back and forth. Even as she watched, the crown of a balding head, wreathed by long strands of grizzled hair, thrust up from the trunk; then a lean, wrinkled face, its beard tangled in the splinters. Cobwebs trailed from its nose and a clump of mushrooms sprouted from one ear. The bright eyes blinked furiously.

"Do you mean to take all day?"

"Who—who are you?" Mallory stammered. "What are you doing in a tree?"

"Obviously, trying my best to get out. First, some idiot with an ax nearly chops off my toes, and now another wants to ask me foolish questions. Merciful moon, am I to be spared nothing?"

A dead branch lay nearby. Mallory seized it and pried at the wood. The tree groaned, ripping and cracking in a shower of bark and splinters. It split in two, spilling its captive onto the ground.

In her first glimpse of him, Mallory saw he wore a moldering leather jacket and a tattered cloak green with moss. Splotches of mildew covered his boots; in his beard hung a number of empty eggshells, and the twigs and leaves of a long-abandoned bird's nest. Before she could reach out to him, the strange being climbed unsteadily to his legs, wiggled his fingers, flexed his arms and beat them against his sides, thereby raising a cloud of midges from the folds of his cloak. He sneezed violently several times; then, heaving sighs of relief, thrust one hand after the other inside his jacket, luxuriously scratching himself.

"Are you—all right?" Mallory asked, uncertain what to say to this odd figure, let alone what to make of him. The old tales told of tree-spirits; but this being, who stood as tall as she did, was of solid, though much withered, flesh.

"Do you have anything to eat?" Without invitation, the freed captive bent down and rummaged through the basket.

"Mushrooms—" began Mallory, about to explain that Mrs. Parsel had fancied some of those delicacies with an omelette that morning. The bearded man, however, had already discovered the contents of the basket and wrinkled his nose in distaste:

"Fungus? No, thank you, I've been living with toadstools long enough."

"There's food in the cook-shop larder," Mallory said. "I'll fetch some for you. The village isn't far."

"Never mind. I shall manage without refreshment." Wrapping his cloak around his shoulders, he started from the clearing.

"Wait," Mallory called, "where are you going? I don't know who you are. I don't even know your name."

The stranger halted. "Arbican."

Mallory frowned. "What's that?"

"Arbican. My name. What use that information may be to you, I cannot imagine. But, since you ask, there it is."

He set off again. Mallory, no better satisfied, hurried after him. "You can't just go away like that, and not another word about who, or why—"

"Young woman," replied Arbican, "let me assure you I have more urgent matters in mind than detailing my life's history. Admittedly, without your help I should still be clamped in that oak tree. If I neglected to express my gratitude sufficiently, then: Thank you, thank you, thank you. Now I suggest you go about your business and I shall go on my way. I foresee difficulties enough in reaching Vale Innis."

"Vale Innis?" cried Mallory. "Why, that's the Land of Heart's Desire—the Happy Land, I know the tale!

In the old days, there was a ship with golden sails; and all the magicians, enchanters, wizards—all sailed away on it. That's why there's none of them left. I only wish they'd stayed."

"I regret to tell you," said Arbican, "one of them did."

"That's not how the story goes," Mallory answered. "I know it by heart. It was the end of magic in the world."

"Oversimplified, but more or less correct," Arbican admitted. "By this time, my colleagues are long gone; unless any had my bad fortune to be shut up in a tree."

Mallory caught her breath. "Colleagues? Do you mean—?"

"I mean I should not be here at all," replied Arbican. "Yes, I am an enchanter. By all rights, I should be in Vale Innis this very moment. In fact, I should have been there ages ago."

"You?" Mallory gasped. "You? An enchanter? But—where's your magic wand? Where's your pointed hat? Your cloak with all the magical signs embroidered on it?"

Arbican rolled up his eyes and puffed his cheeks in a mighty effort to keep his patience. "Would you mind," he said, in a strained voice, "telling me how and where you got such wrongheaded notions?"

"Everyone knows what enchanters look like. In all the tales—"

"I don't know what tales you're talking about," said Arbican. "Idle gossip and rumor, so it sounds to me, fabricated by someone who never saw an enchanter in his life. Pointed hats and embroidered cloaks? I'd feel an utter fool, decked out that way. Enchanters don't need such trappings, though I suppose you mortals might think so. Even in my day, mortals had a deplorable tendency to mix appearance with fact. I should hate to tell you how many numbskulls put crowns on their heads—as if a metal hoop had anything to do with being a king."

"I didn't mean to offend you," said Mallory. "I just thought enchanters would be different, somehow. Or at least they'd be—well, cleaner."

Arbican snorted. "Forgive me for disappointing you. Had I known, I'd have brought along a change of clothing, curled my beard, polished my boots, scented my linen."

"But if you are an enchanter," Mallory went on, "if you were supposed to sail away, then what are you doing here?"

"That's a question I've had ample opportunity to consider," Arbican said. "The answer is: my own fault. I don't deny it, much as I regret it. I was on my way to the harbor when I stopped here to cut myself a walking staff."

"So you got there too late, and the ship sailed without you?"

"Late? I never got there at all. Thanks to the tree. Thanks to the law we had to obey. Oh, I knew about it. I make no excuses. But this was such a small thing.

"The law warned us," Arbican went on, "to leave everything as it was; to interfere with nothing; to harm no living thing. Whoever thought that included a walking staff? The tree was alive, yes; but what harm? It could have spared a branch, it had plenty. So I started cutting one. A deplorable error in judgment. For the tree opened and swallowed me up. Snap! So! I've been there ever since."

"You couldn't have made it open again? Commanded it? Cast a spell?"

"Not while it lived," said Arbican. "A tree draws its strength from the roots of the earth. That's beyond the power of any enchanter."

"It must have been terrible," Mallory said. "When I'm being punished, and Mrs. Parsel locks me in the cellar—I can imagine, being caught inside a tree."

"I doubt it," said Arbican. "You could have no possible conception of how boring it is. Oh, there's a great deal happening; roots, leaves, rind, they all keep busy at their work. But it's the same slow, vegetable sort of business over and over again. One tends to lose interest. To escape unbearable monotony, I put myself in a deep sleep. The ax woke me up. And now, since the tree is dead, my captivity is over."

During Arbican's account, an idea had come to Mallory that made her tremble with such excitement she could barely speak of it. Nevertheless, as soon as Arbican finished, she hastily began:

"About the wishes—"

The enchanter gave her a puzzled glance. "About what wishes?"

"If your tree hadn't been cut down," Mallory answered hesitantly, "that is, if Scrupnor hadn't ordered the woods to be cleared—"

"Scrupnor? What's that?"

15

"He's the new squire," said Mallory. "He owns all this land, and the farms on the other side. He wants to build a road between here and Castleton."

"Fascinating, no doubt, to this what's-his-name," said Arbican, "but hardly of interest to me."

"Yes, it is—I mean, if it hadn't been for Scrupnor's road, your tree wouldn't have been chopped down. Of course, the woodcutters did that. Even so, I was the one who got you out."

"I am quite aware of it. What are you driving at?"

"Three wishes," declared Mallory, plucking up her courage. "In every tale I know, whoever does a good turn to anybody with magical powers—gets three wishes. Please, this is the only chance I'll ever have. I'm asking for mine."

Arbican stared at her a moment, then retorted:

"Three wishes? Why so few? Have a thousand if you like. Granting them—that's another matter. No enchanter in his right mind would grant one wish, let alone three, to a mortal. I shudder to think how you would use them."

"But the tales—" insisted Mallory.

"These tales you keep flinging at me," said Arbican, "believe me, I know nothing whatever about them. I should guess that you humans made them up to suit yourselves, after we had gone. That's the only thing that could account for them. I assure you nothing like that happened in my day. There's a grain of truth, but it's been blown up out of all proportion. Three, indeed, is a magical number—for reasons you couldn't understand and that don't concern you. And you mortals were constantly wishing for things you didn't have. Put the two together, and I can see how such an appalling rumor might start. Wishes? Pure wishful thinking."

Mallory turned her face away, trying to hide her disappointment. "Then you'll grant me nothing—"

"Do you seriously believe anything worthwhile can be had merely for the wishing?" replied Arbican. "Very well, very well, you did me a good turn. You shan't go empty-handed. You shall have a gift, if that will satisfy you; you mortals have such an obsession with getting something in return, that's one thing that hasn't changed. So be it. A small trinket, a remembrance. Here, don't cry. I'll conjure up something for you this very instant."

Grateful for that much, Mallory wiped her cheeks on the back of her hands and watched as Arbican set his cupped palms one on top of the other and muttered under his breath. After a moment, he pulled his upper hand away. Mallory gave him a questioning look. The enchanter's outstretched palm was empty.

Arbican frowned. "One moment. My skill is a little rusty."

Again, he cupped his palms and muttered to himself. He peered between his fingers and his face went even paler:

"Nothing," he said in disbelief. "Nothing at all."

CHAPTER
2

 Staring at his empty hands, Arbican sank down on a clump of grass. Though eager to see a real wizard cast a spell, Mallory was more concerned for Arbican, so shaken by his failure that he seemed unable to speak, as his face clouded and the furrows on his brow deepened.

"It's those wretched years crammed into that tree," he muttered at last. "Something's happened to me. The clumsiest apprentice could have done that charm, but I can't get the hang of it now. It darts away, like a fish in my head. My magic's gone."

"But enchanters can't lose their power. It never happened in any of the tales—"

"More tales? Of course we can lose our power. It seldom happens; but then, one is seldom shut up in a tree. Now, please, I must think this over very carefully."

"You needn't worry about giving me a gift," Mallory suggested. "If it's too much of a strain, I don't want to trouble you."

"Gift?" cried Arbican. "Do you suppose I'm worried about conjuring up some trivial reward? There's more to it than that. I may never get to Vale Innis."

"You've forgotten where it is?"

"No, I haven't forgotten," snapped Arbican. "I mean I can't reach it at all, not in the state I'm in. Without going into details, I put it to you simply: Unless I have all my powers, I'm stuck tighter in your mortal world than ever I was in my tree."

"If you have to stay," said Mallory, "you can surely find something to do. You could learn a trade if you wanted. We need a good stonemason, and there's plenty of work for another carpenter."

"Delightful prospect," said Arbican. "I don't think you realize the situation. In the first place, I don't belong here and I have no desire to linger. In the second place, without my magic I'm helpless as a turtle out of its shell. All I can hope is that my present incapacity is only temporary."

"Until your power comes back," said Mallory, "you could live in the cook-shop." Then she quickly shook her head. "No. Mrs. Parsel won't even let me keep a cat. I can imagine what she'd say if I brought home a wizard. Though I could hide you in the stable for a while."

"And if someone found me there? In my condition, the less mortals see of me the better."

"I know where you'll be safe," Mallory said. "Come with me."

Without waiting for Arbican to question or protest she took his hand and hurried him out of the clearing, half-leading and half-pushing the enchanter through the underbrush. She scrambled down a slope to a shallow gully, while Arbican tried to keep up with her long strides. At last, she stopped where the gully ended in a tumble of rocks, and pointed to the narrow mouth of a cave.

"It's my secret place," Mallory said, drawing the reluctant enchanter after her. "No one in the village knows about it; or if they do, they never bother. Before my father and mother died, the years there was fever in the village, I used to play here all the time. But now, hardly ever. Since the Parsels took me in for their kitchen maid, they keep me too busy. You'll feel right at home."

Arbican glanced around the cave, which widened into a large, rock-walled chamber. He grimaced. "So I should, if I were a bat or a bear."

"Don't enchanters live in caves?" Mallory began. "Or grottoes, or burrows under a hill."

"I am not a rabbit," Arbican replied. "Yes, I do know of one who lived in a cave, but he was a strange sort to begin with. Fascinated with minerals: diamonds, emeralds, all that rubbish. But I assure you his cave was rather more elaborate than this."

"Then you had an enchanted tower?" said Mallory. "A real one, not like my tree—your tree, I should say. I used to play there, too, and climb as high as I could, and make believe I could see all that was happening in the world. Is that what you did?"

"I did nothing of the sort. One hardly needs a tower to know what goes on in the world."

"A castle, then? Is that where you lived? Full of magic mirrors, and chests of jewels, and golden cups? Did you have a high throne of crystal? And servants to fetch you anything you commanded?"

"I lived in a cottage, which suited me very nicely," said Arbican. "You mortals were the ones who put on such airs with your castles. I've never been in one that didn't have a draft howling through it like the north wind."

"I always called this cave my castle," said Mallory.

"It's damp enough," replied Arbican.

"I'd pretend it had golden turrets and banners flying," Mallory went on. "Or make believe it was a great mansion, twice as big as the squire's, and I should be mistress of the manor, with stables of horses, and fine carriages, and lovely gowns; and feather beds; and I should never have to wash dishes or scrub pots. Or if I did, they'd be my own dishes and pots, and not Mrs. Parsel's."

Arbican, pacing over the dirt floor, had stubbed his toe on a heap of smooth pebbles. "What idiot set a pile of rocks in here?" he cried, hopping on one foot. "I'll end up lame if I don't catch my death of chilblains first!"

Mallory stooped to gather up the scattered pebbles. "They're mine," she said. "I used to pretend they were wishing stones. If I held one in my hand, whatever I wished would come true. Of course, it never happened."

"I shouldn't wonder," the enchanter remarked. "Great

heavens, girl, do you mind telling me where you got such peculiar notions of magic?"

"From my mother," answered Mallory.

"Oh, come now," Arbican exclaimed. "You won't have me believe your mother was some kind of enchantress."

"No, she wasn't," Mallory quickly admitted. "But she was a wonderful storyteller; you should have seen how many people in the village would come to listen. But I liked it most when she'd tell the old tales just to my father and me, and there'd be only the three of us beside the fire. My father was a cabinetmaker, the best in the village, and sometimes, when he listened to my mother, he'd carve all sorts of things from bits of wood —birds and beasts, kings and queens, better than any dolls you'd ever see. They had to be burned, after my parents died; Mrs. Parsel was afraid they'd bring fever into her house, too. So, they're gone. But I've never forgotten my mother's tales. I make up my own, too. Maybe that's why they don't sound quite right to you."

"It becomes more and more apparent to me," said Arbican, "you mortals have been both industrious and ingenious in fabricating accounts of matters you know nothing whatever about. And then, in typical human fashion, you've convinced yourselves that such products of your fancy are true, simply because you want them to be true. I suppose it's a harmless occupation, but I find it disconcerting. What a blessing you don't have magical powers! I hate to think what would happen if your wishes were granted: gowns, feather beds, bags of gold, horses and carriages—believe me, if they all came

23

tumbling out of the sky, you'd soon find little pleasure in them. Of all things to wish for, you chose the most useless."

"That's not fair to say," Mallory protested. "You make it sound as though gowns and feather beds were all I cared about. What I wished, more than anything, was for my parents to be alive and all of us happy together."

"As for that," said Arbican, not quite so gruffly, "there has never been enchantment strong enough. Magic can't work miracles."

"One wish did come true," Mallory insisted. "I used to wish for my fairy godmother to come and find me. And here you are."

"Well, I'm certainly not your godmother," retorted Arbican. "And if I don't reach Vale Innis, I'll soon be nothing at all."

"What do you mean?"

"I'll die," Arbican answered flatly. "In short order. I've already lived beyond my time here."

"Why didn't you say so in the first place?" cried Mallory. "That's terrible. Are you sure?"

"Quite sure," answered Arbican.

"How can you say that?" asked Mallory, more dismayed at Arbican's words than the enchanter himself appeared to be. "How can you sit there and talk so calmly about dying?"

"I create illusions," replied Arbican. "I don't indulge myself in them. This is what will happen. I don't say I look forward to it in the least."

"You won't die," Mallory declared. "No, not after I saved your life. I'll help you. I'll do everything I can."

"To think I'd see the day when I have to rely on a mortal," the enchanter groaned. "Ludicrous, incongruous, and a little humiliating. Very well. If I'm to get my powers back again, I shall need a few things: some bread, a piece of cheese, a slice of meat; if possible, a jug of ale."

Mallory frowned. "For a magic potion?"

"For me to eat. In addition to your other misconceptions, do you imagine enchanters don't get hungry?"

Clutching her basket, Mallory hurried from the cave and through the underbrush. At the fringe of the woods, she followed a narrow footpath bordering a new-plowed field; then turned down a sunken lane that led to the first low-roofed houses of the village. Burnet, the weaver, had already opened his shutters and she caught sight of him threading his loom. By this time of day, Emmet the harnessmaker should have been at his work-bench in the open-fronted shop. Instead, the harness-maker and half-a-dozen of the villagers stood intently listening to a man in rough homespun. Mallory recognized him as one of the cottagers who came each week to huckster what they could spare from their vegetable patches. Today, however, the cottager was brandishing a sheet of paper covered with seals and stamps:

"There's the notice," Mallory heard him declare. "See for yourselves. I'm not quick at my letters, but as I make it out, Squire's putting us off the land, and we tenants there since my great-granddad's time."

"Well, Hullock, you can't say nay to him," put in one of the village men. "It's Scrupnor's property now, he has the right side of the law."

"Be damned to him, even so," exclaimed Hullock.

"The old squire would never have done. Not tear down a man's house and home for the sake of a filthy lump of coal. Where do I live then, with wife and little ones?"

"Don't take on," said another of the villagers. "You can lodge with us awhile, till you're settled again."

"And how earn my bread?" cried Hullock. "Grub in Squire's coal pits like a blind mole?"

"It may come to that for us all, sooner or later," answered the villager.

Despite her haste, Mallory stopped to listen. There had been talk, before now, of coal pits to be dug in place of the smallholdings, but no one had really believed Scrupnor would do it. As Mallory stood a moment, the harnessmaker caught sight of her and sadly shook his head.

"I'd wish you a good morning," said Emmet, "but it's far from that. Not for Hullock and his neighbors."

"What, all of them?" asked Mallory, dismayed.

The harnessmaker nodded. "Every one. They've had their notices to vacate. That's not the worst of it, you'll see. This day a year, mark my words, there won't be man, woman, or child who doesn't work for Scrupnor's wages, and he'll call the tune for all of us. Once the road's done, there'll be no need for craftsmen here; not when it's easy to get shoddy goods and ready-mades from Castleton. A blessing your dad's not alive, it would break his heart. Now it won't be the skill in a man's hands that counts, but the money in his pocket."

Mallory dared stay no longer. As much as the harnessmaker's news distressed her, Arbican's needs were the more immediate and urgent. As she turned away, Emmet called after her:

"You watch your step, lass. Mrs. Parsel's been looking for you. Squire's at the cook-shop now, and the notary with him."

Thanks to Emmet's warning, Mallory followed a narrow alley that brought her unseen to the rear of the cook-shop. Scrupnor's bay mare was indeed tethered in the stable, along with two others. Mallory cautiously crossed the yard and ventured to open the back door. Seeing no one in the kitchen, she slipped inside and made her way to the larder.

Beyond the kitchen lay the shop itself, half common room, half parlor. At one of the trestle tables sat Mrs. Parsel in her finest lavender shawl; nearly eclipsed by the stout figure of his wife, Mr. Parsel leaned across the table, cupping his ear as though he feared to miss even one of Scrupnor's words.

 "Now, that settles most of our business," the squire was saying. He picked up the sheets of parchment in front of him and his heavy jaws worked up and down as if he were about to chew the documents, red tapes, wax seals and all. Scrupnor's brass-buttoned riding coat, a black mourning band around one arm, stretched tight across his shoulders; his neck overflowed the linen stock, and he seemed at any moment about to explode out of his clothes. His hair, reddish and short-cropped, scarcely covered all his head, and his bare temples bulged like a pair of clenched fists. "Item, indebtedness. Correct. Item, hypothecation—that's mortgage, Mr. Parsel. The terms are all set forth."

Pulling at his side whiskers, Mr. Parsel nodded eagerly, as if being hypothecated were the dearest wish of his life. Before he could speak, however, Mrs. Parsel heaved herself closer to the table and replied in his place:

"What it agglomerates down to, Squire, our cook-shop's to be made into an inn, and none other in the village. Parsel's to have the keeping of it, him and none other."

"But, now, Squire," Mr. Parsel put in, "as for the meat and drink—the victualization, we call it in the trade—that's to be bought from you?"

"Correct," replied Scrupnor. "In exclusivity, to put the proper legal term on it."

"I've always dealt with Farmer Tench," said Mr. Parsel. "He gives good value for money, especially in the matter of vegetables."

"From now on, you'll deal with me," said Scrupnor. "That, sir, is the very nature and essence of exclusivity."

"Tench won't be happy to lose my trade," said Mr. Parsel, "and he does need the business. If we could make an exception, say, at least, for carrots and parsnips—"

"Squire has better things to think about than carrots and parsnips," Mrs. Parsel broke in, with such a glance at her husband that the inn-keeper-to-be choked off his words and began thoughtfully paring his nails with a tortoiseshell clasp knife.

"Indeed I do, ma'am," said Scrupnor. "Your cook-shop, for one. I mean to have it rebuilt for you. You'll have a new public room, bedchambers, another stable. Once my road's done, it's a straight line between here and Castleton High Road. You'll draw more trade than you ever saw in your life. Your husband will be a rich man, Mrs. P. And a lucky one, on top of it all, with such a helpmeet as you."

A purple blush spread over Mrs. Parsel's cheeks. Though her attempt at a giggle came out more in the way of a snort, she batted her eyes girlishly and from her taut bodice pulled a handkerchief which she fluttered at the squire.

From the kitchen, Mallory could not help overhearing the exchange between the Parsels and Scrupnor; but her thoughts were only to lay hands on whatever leftovers she could find and take them to Arbican as fast as she could. She snatched up half a loaf of bread and a remnant of cheese and dropped them into her basket.

In the common room, Rowan the notary had been sitting a little apart, chewing at the end of a clay pipe. Dark-suited, hair powdered in the old style, he glanced at Scrupnor with a certain air of distaste, then leaned forward in his chair, and said quietly to Mr. Parsel:

"You understand, don't you, Parsel, that Squire holds title to the property. In short, the inn belongs to him until you've paid it off with interest."

Scrupnor turned quickly to the notary. "That's all been gone through. No need for your opinion."

"Hardly an opinion," replied Rowan. "I merely remind Mr. Parsel of the terms as they're drawn up. He has a right to understand his position clearly; indeed, he must give knowing consent."

"He consents," declared Scrupnor. "Leave off with your lawyer's pettifogging." He turned to Mrs. Parsel. "The terms are generous, as you well know. We've agreed on them and so has every tradesman of any account. I don't deny the existence of invidious malcontents. The harnessmaker, for one; the cooper for another. That, ma'am, is their loss if they choose to fall by the wayside, deaf to the voice of progress, blind to the golden vistas of the future. They'll shut up shop by mid-year, I guarantee. Let others more deserving enjoy the blessings of prosperity. Hodge will have a new saw mill and timber yard—naturally, I shall provide the lumber. Burnet shall be cloth merchant in exclusivity, once I've put up my weaving sheds. We'll soon outshine Castleton itself. There won't be a fallow field or a useless bit of woods or a creek that isn't turned to some good purpose. That's progress, ma'am; that's vision."

Scrupnor rolled his eyes upward as if the keenness of such vision could bore through the cook-shop ceiling. Then in a hushed voice of wonder, he added:

"That's coal."

"Coal?" repeated Mr. Parsel, squinting in the same direction as the squire. "Where do you see that?"

"I see it," answered Scrupnor, in a resonating prophetic tone, "gleaming like gold under a threadbare cloak of lead, asking only to be brought into the light. I refer to the land presently rented to the cottagers on the north fields. I've made investigations, had expert reports which confirm what I always knew: that land has better use than to be scraped and scrabbled for crops not worth planting. A blessing for those cottagers, too, in the long run. As soon as the pits are dug, I mean to let them work there, snug underground, out of the wet and weather. Those dirty, drafty kennels they now occupy will be deconstructed. Notice to that effect has been served this very day. In due time, what was a rabble of

idlers will be uplifted to the ranks of honest working-folk, strong of arm, clear of eye, obedient of heart. And thirsty, too, ma'am, which means all the more trade for your inn, at least as concerns the ale house aspect of it."

"Squire," said Mrs. Parsel, "it's an inspiration to hear you speak. I urge you, and in my capacity as presiding officer invite you to address the Ladies' Benevolence. We shall devote an entire evening to your discoursement."

"Gladly," replied Scrupnor, "as soon as my onerous duties allow me that pleasure. Meantime, I look to the Ladies' Benevolence as the hub around which our social graces and good works must revolve."

Hearing this, Mallory made a furious face, since the charitable works of Mrs. Parsel's Ladies' Benevolence consisted mainly in offering each other suppers, accompanied by an ample array of wine bottles, lasting far into the night. Nevertheless, she kept filling her basket. The floor creaked behind her, though before she could turn, an arm was flung tightly about her waist and a hand seized her by the hair.

Mallory choked back a cry and twisted around to find herself staring up into the grinning face of Bolt, the squire's gamekeeper. The more she struggled, the more Bolt tightened his fingers in her hair until her eyes watered so heavily she could scarcely see. She beat her fists against his jacket while Bolt only laughed at her efforts.

"I saw you come sneaking in," he said in her ear, pulling Mallory closer. "Little baggage, what are you up to? You'll catch it from Mrs. P. But you be cheerful and friendly, now; stay on my good side and she'll never know you're here."

For answer, Mallory kicked him twice in the shins. Bolt let out a roar, snatched away his hands to rub frantically at the injured parts, jigging up and down on one leg then the other. The gamekeeper's bellowing, however, brought the Parsels and their company hurrying into the kitchen. Mallory would have tried to escape then and there and face the consequences later. But as the girl stooped to retrieve the scattered leftovers, Mrs. Parsel, showing amazing lightness of foot, laid hold of Mallory and, unhesitatingly, began boxing her ears; alternating gasps of indignation with clucks of apology to Scrupnor.

"Lay on," cried Bolt, as if Mrs. Parsel needed further encouragement.

"My dear," Mr. Parsel murmured to his wife, "shouldn't we know what she's done?"

"She's like to paralyze me, the little beast, isn't that enough?" the gamekeeper declared.

"Quite enough," agreed Mrs. Parsel, never missing a stroke. "You stay out of this, Parsel. She's in one of her fits. If you ask me, it's the fairy tales that does it. Her head's so stuffed with those tales; I try every way to beat them out, but no use."

"Pernicious and unwholesome," said Scrupnor nodding gravely, while Bolt limped to the kitchen table and sat down. "A heavy burden you bear, Mrs. Parsel. But I fear not much can be done. Once these fancies infect the brain, they're not easily cured. I tell you, Mrs. Parsel, I'd rather a dozen cases of the smallpox than one case of the fairy tales."

"It's in her blood," said Mrs. Parsel. "Handed down from her mother, as you might say a family curse."

"I always enjoyed hearing the old stories," Mr. Parsel murmured.

"Yes, and you see what they've done to you," retorted Mrs. Parsel. "Turned you into a softheaded fool. If it hadn't been for my pushing and prodding, you'd have never seen what a fortune Squire offered you. Brace yourself up, Parsel. Drain such nonsense out of your mind. Why, that girl's downright contagious!"

Mrs. Parsel had meanwhile finished her duties with Mallory. "Now, then," she said, in a tone promising further ministrations at a more convenient time, "set out glasses, and that bottle of port wine for Squire. And a plate of cakes. Make a nice tray, do you hear, with the clean napkins."

Though her ears rang and her cheeks smarted, Mallory forced herself to stay silent, for the sake of avoiding any more delay in returning to Arbican. Inwardly, however, she raged and wept, and wished for even the smallest portion of the enchanter's magical powers. "I'd put a spell on her she'd not forget," Mallory said to herself. "Let her break out in boils! In warts! In toothaches!" Furiously, she seized goblets and silverware from the cupboard, threw them onto the tray, and set down the wine bottle with such a jolt that the knives and forks danced into the air.

Crediting Mallory's energy and haste to the salutary effect of the ear-boxing, Mrs. Parsel bobbed her head in satisfaction; then, laying a hand on Scrupnor's arm, drew him toward the table:

"Come, Squire, partake a little refreshment of that

35

port wine. I'll even swallow a drop of it myself, as I need revivifying. You can't believe the effort of training such a creature. That girl will be the exhaustion of me, and the sorrow of my days. But you have your own griefs and sorrows, Squire, as to which we are very condolative."

"Thank you, Mrs. Parsel," Scrupnor answered solemnly. "I find your sympathy very heartening in my bereavement."

"You bear your loss with such courage, and set the example to us all," said Mrs. Parsel. "Poor Mr. Sorrel. How you must grieve for him. But I tell you, Squire, he'll never rest easy in his grave until his heartless assassinator comes to the bar of justice."

"Nor will I rest easy," declared Scrupnor, with a sigh. "I was his bailiff, his confidential clerk; no more, you might say, than engaged in a fiduciary relationship. Remuneration per annum. Hired and paid. That's the cold way of putting it. But I tell you there was a filial affection nothing less than paternal between I and that blessed old man. I couldn't have been fonder of Squire Sorrel if he was my own father.

"I recriminate myself," Scrupnor went on. "I should never have gone to Castleton. The business could have waited. I should have been at his side. Not a moment of the day passes, but I wish I had stayed with him."

"There, there, Squire," said Mrs. Parsel, as Scrupnor bowed his head so deeply that his chin vanished into the folds of his neckcloth. "I know it's hard for we sensitive souls not to suffer from our feelings. Damn that little slut, where's the wine?"

"The deplorable event has incinerated itself forever in my memory," said Scrupnor. "I still tremble at the recollection, though it's already a month gone by. I came back from Castleton, business done to the old squire's profit. But all useless. All shattered. The servant girls beside themselves. The master smothered with a pillow in his very bed."

"We're none of us safe in our beds nowadays," Mr. Parsel observed. "Highwaymen, footpads, cutthroats, every sort of desperate fellow lurking about."

"It must have been one such vagabond," replied Scrupnor. "There was a ladder against the wall, the window broken open. A heinous crime, sir, not to mention purloinment of valuables. I'm not ashamed to admit I was so sick at heart I could hardly swallow my breakfast; and lone and lorn as if I was an orphan."

"A sad loss," the notary agreed, in a dry voice. "Yet not without its compensations, wouldn't you say, Squire? For you did come into the manor house, tenant farms; in fine, all Sorrel Holdings—rather, Scrupnor Holdings, as you call it now."

Scrupnor reddened and for the instant it seemed he might have some hard words for the notary, who continued puffing on his pipe. However, he recovered himself and said:

"Yes, Rowan, I did shoulder that burden, as he had always insisted I do. How many times did he beg me to take possession of the Holdings after he was gone, as his reward to a good and faithful steward? And how many times did I tell him the privilege of his association was reward enough for me? But no, he must have his own way and set it down in his will. I pleaded with him not to lay such a responsibility on me; but there was no one else, not an offspring, not kith nor kin did he have in all the world. So, for his sake, I mean to make the Holdings prosper, no matter what the toil and labor it may cost me. It's my duty, nothing less will answer."

"Squire," said Mrs. Parsel, "you're one of nature's noblemen. It's a pleasure to hear you talk of duty, that's a word seldom spoken in these times. But have a care; you're too unselfish for your own good."

"I know it," sighed Scrupnor. "I know it, but I can't help it. That's my nature. I've already offered a thousand gold sovereigns for the apprehension of that cold-blooded murderer. Well, Mrs. Parsel, I say this to you— and let Rowan here bear witness to it—I'll pledge more than that. Whoever puts the old squire's killer into my hands, in pure gratitude I'd give him the Holdings, every bit of them, and never grudge an acre."

Mr. Parsel blinked at the magnitude of such an offer, and Mrs. Parsel shook her head in admiration:

"There speaks a full heart, Squire. There's generosity, pure as gold."

"No, ma'am," said Scrupnor, "only a devotion to justice. The Holdings? Mere worldly goods. They count not a snap, Mrs. P., compared with avenging the demise of my dearest friend and master."

"You can't be serious, Squire," said Rowan. "The reward is ample as it stands. No need to let yourself be carried away by your grief."

"Do you question my sincerity?" Scrupnor angrily retorted. "I'd give up the Holdings without a second thought, and give still more, if it could only resuscitate the dear departed and have him walk among us once again."

"For shame, Mr. Rowan," said Mrs. Parsel. "Shame on you for doubting Squire's word."

"Ma'am, I don't doubt it for a moment," answered Rowan. "I simply point out that we say things in the grip of strong emotions that we should be wiser to forget about in later calm reflection."

"That's not the way of it with Squire," declared Mrs. Parsel. "When he says a thing, he means it, permanent and for all times. When he says he'd give the Holdings as a reward—why, so he would, there's no question in my mind. You could set that down on paper, signed and sealed." She turned to Scrupnor. "Isn't that so, Squire?"

"Eh?" said Scrupnor, a little uncomfortably. "Why, yes, naturally, so I would. But a man's word is his bond, there's no need for anything else."

Rowan shook his head. "In point of law, there should indeed be a formal document."

"And Squire would put his name to it as quick as he could take pen in hand," Mrs. Parsel declared. "This very instant, if he had the occasion."

"True, Mrs. P., absolutely," said Scrupnor, shifting in his chair. "And now, alas, I must be on my way. Business presses, you understand."

"There, Mr. Rowan, there you hear him," Mrs. Parsel triumphantly cried. "You could draw up whatever document you choose, even as you sit here. You see, notary, how you've misjudged the size of Squire's heart! A greater spirit than any of us."

Rowan shrugged. "Well, the matter is simple

enough. I have my seal and stamp with me. I can draw up a formal statement easily enough—if the Squire's inclined to have me do it."

"No cause for precipitative haste," said Scrupnor. "Moderation and measure in all things. I'll get around to it in due course."

"Ah, Squire, do it now," urged Mrs. Parsel. "Allow me the joy of seeing you give the lie to any man who'd cast such a doubt on your nature."

Scrupnor drew a heavy breath, then nodded briskly at Mrs. Parsel and at the notary, who had already taken a sheet of legal paper from his writing case. "Very well. It will be a pleasure. A further gesture of my esteem for the dear departed— Yes, by all means, write it down. Get one with it, Rowan," he muttered through his teeth. "I've better things to do than waste time on lawyer's quibblings."

CHAPTER
4

 Scrupnor had put the last flourish
to his signature when Mallory brought in the tray. Mrs.
Parsel was beaming, enraptured at this new evidence of
the Squire's selflessness, but her expression instantly
changed at sight of her kitchen maid and she rapped
angrily on the table:

"The cakes, girl! What have you done with them?"

Mallory flew to the kitchen and hurried back with
the forgotten plate. Mrs. Parsel, meanwhile, had picked
up the wine bottle to fill the squire's glass; but she
halted in mid course:

"Stupid wench! Where's your head this morning?
You've not drawn the cork!"

Mallory again sped to the kitchen, returned with the
corkscrew, and tried as fast as she could to open the
bottle. The harder she pulled and twisted, however, the
tighter the cork wedged itself in the neck; until at last it

41

suddenly came loose, the bottle slipped from her hands and shattered on the floor, splashing wine over Mrs. Parsel's slippers and the hem of her gown.

"That girl will ruin us!" cried Mrs. Parsel, as Mallory scurried for the mop and dustpan. "She'll destroy us with her idiocy! Clean up the mess you've made this instant! Fetch another bottle!"

Scrupnor, however, rose to his feet. "No, no thank you, Mrs. P. I should not have indulged myself in your hospitality so long to begin with."

While Rowan put the document into his writing case, the squire strode to the kitchen doorway and ordered Bolt to bring around the horses. Mrs. Parsel smiled and curtsied after the departing Scrupnor, so deeply moved by this morning's business he could scarcely wait to put it behind him. No sooner were the visitors out of sight than Mrs. Parsel turned furiously to Mallory, hastily mopping up the puddle:

"You've put us out the price of a bottle of wine, and who's to pay for it? If you had wages, I'd stop them this moment!"

Mallory braced herself for another box on the ear, clenched her teeth, and fortified herself by adding a seven-year itch to the other afflictions she wished for her benefactress. But Mrs. Parsel had settled on a longer method of correction.

"You'll launder my gown and clean my slippers, though you've spoiled them past wearing. And have it done by mid-day. You'll scrub that floor, too, and don't let me find speck nor spot. When you've finished that—"

The more Mrs. Parsel added to the list of tasks, the

more Mallory despaired, seeing herself trapped for hours in the cook-shop. Arbican, she was sure, had already begun to worry about her ever coming back.

"Don't stand there like a dumb ox," cried Mrs. Parsel. "You've already idled away the morning. Get to work straightaway. I'll have my eye on you."

Meanwhile, Mr. Parsel, still holding his unfilled glass, had been wistfully looking at the wreckage of the wine bottle, sure his wife would never agree to open another merely for his personal refreshment now the squire had gone. To console himself for lost opportunity, Mr. Parsel ventured to nibble at the rejected cakes.

"Look here," he said, taking a pair of yellow gloves from the table. "Squire's forgotten these."

"Couldn't you have seen that before he went?" replied Mrs. Parsel, shifting her attention from Mallory to her husband. "You're as harebrained as the girl, I swear you are. Squire will be wanting those gloves."

"He'll no doubt send for them once he remembers where he left them," said Mr. Parsel. "He won't freeze in the meantime."

Mrs. Parsel turned to Mallory. "You run to the Holdings. Give those gloves to Squire with our compliments and tell him as we're sorry for his inconvenience."

"My dear," put in Mr. Parsel, "that's a dreadful way to go on foot. She'll be fairly worn out by the time she's back. I can saddle the horse and ride there—"

"Horse?" exclaimed Mrs. Parsel. "And have the beast work up more appetite? Is that how you mean to waste your fortune? On oats for that lazy, spavined creature? He'll go to the boneyard as soon as the inn

44

turns a profit. Horse, indeed! The girl has stronger legs and sounder wind."

Mr. Parsel gave Mallory a rueful glance and shrugged his shoulders helplessly. Mrs. Parsel, as an afterthought, took the cakes out of her husband's reach. Wrapping the dainties in a napkin, she set them carefully in a wicker hamper and, from the pantry shelf, added a fresh-baked pork pie and a pot of strawberry jam.

"You'll give Squire this, too," she told Mallory. "Poor man, he's so busy seeing to others' welfare, he scarcely has a moment to enjoy the better things in life. He'll appreciate a little thoughtfulness; and it should put him in mind to give us a cheaper price on vegetables."

She thrust the hamper into Mallory's arms. "Be off, now, and quick. I want to see you back here within the hour."

After a parting shove from her benefactress to set her on the way, Mallory hurried from the shop. Mrs. Parsel, she realized furiously, had given her an impossible task. "And she's done it on purpose, too," Mallory told herself. "There's no way in the world I can get to the Holdings and back in an hour, not even if I run every step. Oh, blast Scrupnor and his stupid gloves!"

Nevertheless, she also realized Mrs. Parsel had unwittingly provided her with food of better quality and quantity than she herself could have scraped together from leftovers; and she had no intention of putting this windfall into the hands of Scrupnor. Arbican, she decided, needed nourishment far more urgently than the squire. What Mrs. Parsel would do to her, once she

45

learned the tidbits had never reached their proper destination, Mallory could easily imagine.

"I don't care," she told herself defiantly. "Arbican's *my* enchanter."

Still, she had been delayed longer than she had foreseen, and her concern for the enchanter gave fresh speed to her steps. She passed quickly through the village, fearful of being further hindered; but soon saw she had nothing to worry about on that score. The streets were empty and silent, as if the cottagers' misfortune had spread its gloom to all the other houses.

Beyond the village, instead of following the lane to the Holdings, Mallory turned and ran into the trees. However, at last reaching the cave, she halted in alarm at the loud rasping and snorting noises. With a cry, ready to defend the helpless wizard against whatever monstrous attack, she plunged inside and nearly tripped over Arbican, who lay flat on his back. She flung down the hamper and dropped to her knees beside him. Only then did she realize he was merely fast asleep and snoring at the top of his lungs.

She gave a sob of relief. Arbican stirred, opened one eye, then the other, and sat up:

"So there you are. I must say you took your time about it."

Mallory had been so certain Arbican would be as worried about her as she was about him that his casual remark stung more sharply than Mrs. Parsel's box on the ear. For the instant, forgetting he was an enchanter, she retorted:

"I've only just run my legs off. And torn my dress. It was all I could do to get back to you, and I shouldn't

46

even be here but on my way to the Holdings, and I'll be punished for that. And you, snoring away as if nothing else mattered!"

"First, I do not snore," answered Arbican, drawing himself up, "and second—"

"You do!" insisted Mallory. "I heard you. It was terrible."

"I was thinking," said Arbican. "Loudly, perhaps. But thinking, nonetheless. And second, much as I regret your difficulties I must regard them as rather less distressing than my own. A torn dress can easily be mended, hardly a matter of life and death."

"I'm sorry," said Mallory, though disappointed at Arbican's response. He was right, as she admitted; but she still wished he had given her a warmer welcome. "It wasn't only on my account. There was bad news in the village. Scrupnor's tearing down all the cottages and he's going to start a coal pit. I doubt that means much to you, either. I don't suppose you know or even care what coal is."

"I know perfectly well," said Arbican. "We enchanters were quite aware of it. And in our considered opinion, it was best left where it was. If you mortals happened to stumble on it, well, then, the responsibility was yours. But we surely weren't going to encourage it. What happened, with coal or anything else, was altogether up to you."

"How could that be? You were the ones to decide things, weren't you? With all you knew, and all your magical powers—why, the greatest kings and queens had to obey your commands."

"Another of your peculiar notions," Arbican said.

"No, not at all. You humans were free to do as you chose and take the consequences. Of course we had power; but we weren't about to use it at every whip-stitch, to pull you out of messes you made for your-selves. Of course we had wisdom—if anyone chose to seek it from us; needless to say, few did. But we weren't going to cram it down people's throats. That, in itself, would hardly be very wise."

"If that's so," began Mallory, frowning, "it sounds as if magic didn't make much difference to anybody."

The enchanter nodded. "That's the first flicker of true intelligence I've observed in you since we met. Much difference? None at all. Why do you think our age ended? Because our magic failed. I told you before, magic can't work miracles; you humans have to work your own. There was no enchantment to make you the least bit kinder, gentler, or happier. Without that, there was no point in it."

"Do you mean you never changed pumpkins into coaches? Or spun straw into gold?"

"Oh, I don't say *never*," admitted Arbican. "It would depend on the situation. We were perfectly capable of doing so; but hardly for the sake of satisfying the greed of some lout who wanted to enrich himself. Or a king who wanted the upper hand on his neighbors. They managed that quite well on their own. Shape-changing, transmutation, and the rest—we did that only to help you understand: the world is all one place, life is life, whatever form it happens to be in. A simple proposition, but one you mortals found equally simple to ignore. Our efforts turned out to be useless."

"Useless?" said Mallory. "If I had your powers, you'd see if they were useless. For one thing, I'd soon put an end to Scrupnor's coal pits. I'd turn the coal to dust; or the picks and shovels to glass, so they'd always break. You didn't have the coal mines in your day, you said so yourself. But Emmet, the harnessmaker, saw one in King's Mickle, when he went visiting his cousin. The town's filthy, you can hardly breathe. Most of the people work in the shafts, but they're poorer than before, and worse off than ever. And there was a man had his arm torn off when the steam engine exploded—"

"The what-engine?"

"Steam engine," said Mallory, and tried to describe it as well as she could, without understanding much of it herself. "It's a new invention, Emmet says. It boils water and turns wheels."

"And, apparently, explodes from time to time."

"It's very dangerous," Mallory said. "It's supposed to save work, but Emmet says the folk in King's Mickle work twice as hard just to keep in running. He says it does more harm than good. The steam engine—yes, that's something you wouldn't know about."

"Luckily," said Arbican. "It would have given me nightmares. This engine of yours, it doesn't have a mind of its own, does it? Of course not. You mortals thought it up. You built it. Therefore, if it does any harm, blame yourselves, not the machine. Instead of complaining, do something about it."

"That's easy for you to say," Mallory answered. "You have magical powers. We don't. Nobody can do anything about Scrupnor. I certainly can't. But I could, if you'd show me how to use magic on him; cast a spell and put him to sleep for a thousand years—"

"You've understood nothing at all of what I've been telling you," said Arbican. "Magic doesn't touch the real center of things, only the outside edges. Suppose, indeed, you put this fellow Scrupnor out of the way? What's the good, if you keep on making the same mistakes over and over again? You don't cure an itch merely by scratching it."

"I don't care," said Mallory. "I still wish I could change him into a toad, or send him flying to the moon."

"Nonsense," replied Arbican. "No need for that. You have power enough already to do anything you want, if you really want to do it."

"But you just finished telling me that magic was useless," Mallory protested.

"I said 'magic' not 'power,'" corrected Arbican. "As far as power is concerned, you mortals have precisely the same powers as the greatest enchanter. Only yours take a different shape. And most of the time, you don't even realize you have them. You're so busy wishing for good fortune you don't have time to find it for yourselves."

Mallory, still puzzled and unconvinced, would have asked Arbican to tell her more. The enchanter, however, had discovered the provisions in the hamper and was cramming bits of pie into his mouth.

"You deal with your problems in your way," mumbled the enchanter, trying to chew and talk at the same time, "and I shall deal with mine. While you insisted I was snoring, I was devising a plan for getting myself to Vale Innis."

"You found a way?"

"Of course," replied Arbican. "Very simple. I should have thought of it immediately. I shall sail there by boat, as I should have done in the first place."

"No one in the village has a sailboat," said Mallory. "There's a barge at the timber yard by the river. Hodge uses it to ferry logs. There's a couple of rowboats, and that's all."

"No common craft will take me to Vale Innis," the enchanter said. "I shall build my own, and build it from the wood of my oak tree. As it was my prison, it shall be my vessel of freedom. During all those years, no doubt some of my own magic seeped into the wood, and that should make it all the better."

"Have you ever built a boat?" asked Mallory.

"No," said Arbican. "Nor have I ever stood on my ear, or caught eels in a sieve. Given the situation, I shall know how to deal with it."

CHAPTER
5

 Swallowing the last morsels of food, Arbican climbed to his feet and brushed the crumbs from his beard. His cheeks, Mallory was glad to see, had turned a healthy pink and his eyes had brightened. She followed as the enchanter stepped briskly out of the cave and made his way back to the fallen oak.

"Are you going to build the boat now?" asked Mallory, as Arbican critically eyed the tree. "Just like that? Shouldn't you have a magic wand? Or draw a magic circle, and burn roots and herbs?"

"Certainly not," Arbican snorted. "For some strange reason, you humans have always had the notion that anything important must be accompanied by a great show of nonsense. In my day, there were those who wouldn't believe the simplest weather prophecy unless we made a to-do over it. Somehow, it reassured them.

Inessential, nevertheless. The magic is inside, not outside. Now, you mentioned a river. Which way?"

Mallory pointed the direction. Arbican then fixed his gaze on the tree trunk, stretched out his hands, and began murmuring under his breath.

"Wait—please," Mallory suddenly burst out. "I must ask you—"

"Will you be quiet!" ordered the enchanter, frowning in exasperation. "My power had just started working. Very well, what is it now?"

"Please—" urged Mallory. "Take me with you. To Vale Innis—"

"What?" cried Arbican, staring at her as if he could hardly believe his ears. "You? A mortal? Great heavens, girl, that's impossible."

"For an enchanter? It can't be impossible," Mallory insisted. "Surely you could do it if you wanted? It's bad enough drudging for the Parsels, but if Scrupnor has his way, it's going to be worse; for the whole village, too."

"So you, for one, prefer to run off? While the others make the best of a bad bargain? You humans haven't changed at all since my day, have you?"

"I didn't mean it that way," Mallory protested.

"However you meant it," said Arbican, "it's out of the question. No, I could not take you with me even if I wanted to. Absolutely not. So put that idea out of your head, once and for all."

Mallory lowered her eyes; more than disappointed, she now felt foolish at having made such a plea. Worse, Arbican had judged her selfish, and she wondered if he had been right. Arbican, meanwhile, seemed to bend under some heavy but invisible burden. The tree remained as it was and after several moments Mallory ventured to whisper:

"What's wrong? It isn't turning into a boat."

"Of course it isn't," snapped Arbican. "Only an idiot would build a boat in the middle of the woods. I shall raise this tree and have it fly to the river. Now, if holding your tongue is too difficult for you, kindly go and wait somewhere else."

He turned again to his task. His arms tensed and trembled while droplets trickled down his forehead into his beard. The tree rocked back and forth, slowly rose a hand's breadth above the turf, only to fall heavily to the ground.

Arbican grunted and puffed out his cheeks. He seemed, suddenly, to have grown taller than Mallory. Then she realized the enchanter, not the oak, was rising steadily into the air.

"Catch hold!" shouted Arbican, waving his arms and kicking his heels. "The spell's gone wrong! Pull me down! Can't you see I'm floating away?"

Mallory sprang forward, leaped as high as she could, and snatched at Arbican's feet, already beyond her grasp. Sputtering and flapping his cloak, the enchanter continued his flight.

Then, even as she watched helplessly, the enchanter's waving arms blurred and shimmered. Mallory rubbed her eyes. Within the instant, so quickly that one shape seemed to flicker into the other, Arbican was gone and in his place, awkwardly flapping its wings, was a large gray goose.

The bird stretched its neck and beat its wings, as if

finding some difficulty in staying aloft. It hung briefly poised in the air before plunging to the ground, where it landed in a burst of feathers.

"Now this is intolerable," came a voice from the goose's bill, which clacked open and shut irritably. "I haven't flown for ages. Am I expected to do it at a moment's notice?"

"You turned yourself into a goose," Mallory gasped, still unable to believe her eyes.

"Most assuredly I did not," replied Arbican. "I had nothing to do with it. Do you think I deliberately chose this shape? My powers are all topsy-turvy. I can't manage them. All I wanted to do was float back to earth— and you see the consequences."

"But you can't stay that way," said Mallory. Her first shock had passed and she was growing a little more used to conversing with a goose; though she had to remind herself continually that it was no bird at all, but the enchanter merely in a different guise. "What are you going to do? Wait, I know," she hurried on, brightening. "When the princess kissed the frog, he turned back into a prince. Do you think if I—"

"No, I do not," returned Arbican, with a honking kind of snort. "That's more of your fairy tales; it has no bearing whatever on the facts of the matter."

"I only thought it might help," answered Mallory, wounded. "But if that's the way you feel about it—"

"Feelings have nothing to do with the case," said Arbican. "It will take more than a kiss to get me out of this bundle of feathers. If I can't control my power, I may be stuck here as badly as I was in my tree. Though

I must say between the two I'd rather be a bird than a vegetable."

"If you can't change yourself back," asked Mallory, "then do you think you could fly to Vale Innis? You wouldn't need the boat at all."

The goose unfolded a wing and cocked a thoughtful eye at it. "Perhaps you're right. I should hate admitting to my colleagues that I couldn't handle the most elementary transformation; I'd never hear the end of it. Still, that's better than staying in your world.

"Yes, I'm sure I can," the enchanter went on, stretching his wings and rising on his webbed feet as if to take flight then and there. "These geese are strong creatures, you know. Good thing I didn't end up as a chicken. Yes, I believe this will do perfectly. So, I shall be on my way. Goodby, I wish you well. 'Wish'—that's a hope, you understand, not a promise."

Mallory, more unsettled by the enchanter's abrupt leave-taking than by his transformation, could only stammer a confused farewell, adding, "Watch out for hawks—"

"The hawks," Arbican assured her, "had better watch out for me."

With that, he beat his wings vigorously, launched himself into the air, and began climbing steadily upward. Forlorn, Mallory watched his flight. However, at the level of the tree tops, the goose veered sharply, seeming to struggle against the wind. Instead of gaining height, the bird labored mightily to keep aloft. Mallory cried out in dismay as it plummeted earthward. For it was no longer a goose, but Arbican, once again in his own shape, frantically waving his arms and kicking his legs.

An instant later, the enchanter went crashing heavily through the upper limbs of a high elm and vanished into the foliage. Mallory raced to the tree. Caught among the branches like a fly in a web, Arbican dangled head downward, one leg flung over a jutting limb, his beard ensnared by twigs. The enchanter's face was crimson, a result of both his posture and his indignation.

"Don't move!" ordered Mallory, scrambling up the trunk. "Stay right as you are."

"Can I do anything else?" flung back the enchanter. "Except fall and break my neck?"

By this time, Mallory had succeeded in climbing close enough to disentangle Arbican's beard. To do more, she realized, would be difficult; for Arbican was so ensnared that a false move on his part might send him tumbling head first to the ground. The enchanter's predicament had done nothing to improve his temper; while Mallory tried to study the best way to get him down, Arbican sputtered and fumed, until at last Mallory lost her own patience:

"Will you be quiet?" she burst out. "The way you're carrying on, you'll only make things worse. Now, move very slowly and do exactly as I tell you. Or you will break your neck, and mine too."

Cautiously, she hoisted herself to the branch nearest the enchanter, who still grumbled under his breath. From there, she was able to unhook his leg while Arbican, obediently following her directions, took a firm grasp on the limb just below him. As Mallory ordered, he swung down until he was able to clamp his knees against the trunk. Inch by inch, as she pointed out each handhold, Arbican climbed gingerly to the ground. Out of breath, trembling from his exertions, he collapsed in a heap, while Mallory clambered after him. The enchanter, for once too exhausted even to complain, held his head in his hands. The branches had torn his cloak and pulled away bits of his beard; and the only reminder of his hopeful flight was a ragged feather clinging to his disheveled hair.

"Whatever happened?" asked Mallory, once sure the enchanter had been wounded only in his dignity. "You were doing so well."

"I told you I'm not master of my powers," Arbican replied. "They come and go as they please. I can't get hold of them. Fly to Vale Innis? I doubt I'll ever get there at all."

"You can still try to sail," Mallory reminded him.

"Build a boat? The way my spells are going, it would turn out to be a wheelbarrow."

"Suppose you built it the ordinary way? Mr. Parsel keeps a box of tools in the shed. I could bring them here. The oak has all the wood we need. For a sail, we can use a bedsheet; or one of Mrs. Parsel's petticoats, they're certainly big enough."

"A fine figure I'd cut," said Arbican, "sailing to Vale Innis, propelled by bed linen and underclothing. However, this is no time to be picky about details. Very well. First, how do you propose to get this tree to the river?"

"We'll have to saw off the branches, to begin with," answered Mallory. "That should make it easier to handle. Between the two of us, we can drag it with ropes."

"Delightful," grumbled Arbican. "You mortals may be used to that kind of work; I'm not. All I see coming out of your scheme is a sprained back and blistered fingers."

"Well, I'm sorry," returned Mallory, "I want to help you, but if a few blisters are going to bother you, there's nothing to be done."

"I'm afraid that may be the case," said Arbican, looking gloomier than ever. "It also occurs to me it will take too long. I need a seaworthy ship, not a raft. We could spend weeks, even longer. I doubt I have that much time left to me."

"Even so, we could still try," Mallory urged. "Meanwhile, your powers might come back again, just as they used to be."

"And if they don't?"

"You'd be no worse off than you are now. We have to do something, don't we? There's no use going round in circles. Now, the first thing is to get some rope—"

"Stop, stop," said Arbican. "I'm trying to think. What was it you said—?"

"Rope. We can tie it around the trunk—"

"No, not that. Wait, I have it. Circles." He stopped short for a moment, frowned and rubbed his brow. "It's in the back of my mind. I'd forgotten. Living in a tree makes the memory rather wooden." Suddenly his face brightened. "Yes, yes, of course! The circle of gold!"

CHAPTER
6

 Arbican jumped to his feet, more excited than Mallory had ever seen him. "That's it! The simplest thing in the world!"

"A circle of gold?" said Mallory. "I don't understand—"

"The spell, the incantation, the recipe, whatever you want to call it. Every apprentice learns it in case of emergency. To think it had slipped my mind! No matter, I have it now: *To gain all power lost of old, a maid must give a circle of gold.*"

"I still don't understand what it means."

"It means," answered Arbican, "exactly what it says. What a relief. That clears up things considerably. Now, once I find a maid—"

"Why not me?" asked Mallory. "I'm a maid, aren't I? If you tell me what I have to do—"

"A maid," said Arbican, "is not, in these terms,

associated with kitchens. Thank you, nonetheless, for your offer."

"Whatever sort of maid you're thinking of," said Mallory, "I'm sure I must be one."

Arbican said nothing for a moment, then nodded. "Yes, you might do very well for that part of it. That leaves only the circle of gold to be accounted for."

"What kind of circle?"

"What difference does it make? A circle is a circle, isn't it? The spell says no more than that. You should have no trouble finding something appropriate. I shan't keep it. You'll get it back, after it serves its purpose."

"It must have been easier in your day," said Mallory. "There's no gold to speak of in the village. I surely haven't any. My mother's wedding ring—Mrs. Parsel sold it long ago. Mrs. Parsel? She wears a ring. Whether it's really gold, I don't know. Besides, she never takes it off; her finger's grown too thick."

"Do you mean to tell me," said Arbican, "for lack of a mere trinket, my spell is ruined? Unthinkable!"

"Scrupnor might have something we could use," Mallory went on. "But how to find it?" She gave a cry of dismay. "Scrupnor! The gloves!"

"We're talking about gold," said Arbican, "not gloves."

"They're Scrupnor's. He left them at the shop. I forgot. I was to take them to the Holdings."

"He can get along without them," said Arbican. "Don't waste time on pointless errands."

"I must," Mallory insisted. "It's bad enough you ate all the food Mrs. Parsel meant for him. If she knows I didn't even bring his gloves to him, she'll lock me up for days. I'll never get away to help you."

"In that case, deliver the wretched things and have done with it."

"It's too late. She only gave me an hour, and that wasn't enough to begin with. I was in trouble when I left, now I'll be in worse."

"And so will I," said Arbican, tugging angrily at his beard. "Thanks to some fool and his gloves. Very well, I'll try to carry you to what's-his-name, Scrupnor, and bring you back to this Parsel creature as fast as I can."

"Carry me?" returned Mallory. "You'd never get half way."

"Not on my back," snapped Arbican. "Do you take me for a pack mule? No, I'll try my power again. If it works, we'll be there in a wink. If it doesn't, we might not move from this spot, or we might end up who knows where. There's a risk, I warn you."

"I'm not afraid," Mallory declared in spite of the sudden trembling of her knees. However, the prospect of being separated from Arbican brought back much of her courage. "Tell me what I have to do."

"You'll guide me," said Arbican, taking one of her hands firmly in his own. "Think where you want to go. See it behind your eyes and inside your head. Can you do that?"

"I don't know. I'll try. I haven't been often to the Holdings."

"Do your best, then."

Mallory shut her eyes tightly, remembering as clearly as she could the last time she had ridden there with

Mr. Parsel in the horse cart. She pictured to herself the high wall of gray stone, the iron gate, the gravel pathway curving in front of the mansion; the tall chimneys, the gables, the casements. However, no sooner did these come to mind than a dozen other recollections flooded over them. The more she tried to fix the Holdings in her imagination, the more her thoughts flew elsewhere: to Scrupnor, the broken wine bottle, to Arbican caught in the tree. She heard the enchanter's voice:

"Ready?"

"It makes my head spin," cried Mallory. "I'm trying as hard as I can, but everything's mixed up."

"You're trying too hard. Hold your thoughts gently, don't squeeze the life out of them."

Mallory's vision of the Holdings reappeared, but along with it came Mrs. Parsel threatening to lock her in the cellar; and she saw herself beating vainly against a bolted door.

"Now!" commanded Arbican.

"Wait—not yet!" Mallory's heart pounded, her ears rang as the turf gave way beneath her feet. Clutching the hamper, she felt herself go blindly lurching and spinning through sudden blackness. Arbican still held her hand; but now, to keep from falling, she clung to the latch of a heavy, iron-studded portal. Beside her, the enchanter peered curiously around the windowless room at the shelves loaded with stacks of papers and boxes tied with cord. In one corner stood a writing desk and a high stool. At a table, hedged with account books, a large metal cashbox by his elbow, sat Scrupnor.

The squire at that moment glanced up from the ledger in which he had been writing a column of figures.

He reached out to dip his quill into the ink pot; but at sight of Mallory and Arbican he stopped his hand in mid-air. His eyes bulged, his cheeks twitched with a life of their own, and he sprang to his feet, overturning the cashbox and sending the ink pot flying.

Her head still whirling, startled no less than Scrupnor to find herself in the squire's counting room, Mallory blurted out the first words that came to her lips:

"You—you forgot your gloves."

Scrupnor had flung out his arms as though to ward off what he supposed could only be some fiendish assault on his person and possessions; but the sound of Mallory's voice seemed to assure him that he had to deal with beings of flesh and blood. His fear turned to fury as he roared at her:

"How did you come here? What are you up to, spying on me?"

"It's cakes—and a pork pie," stammered Mallory. "They've been eaten. I'm sorry. Your gloves—"

"Pork pie? Gloves be damned! What have you seen, you little slut? Answer me that!" Instead of calming, the squire's rage flamed higher; he seized Mallory and would have thrown her to the floor had Arbican not stepped forward and commanded him to stop. The enchanter raised an arm and pointed a skinny finger at the furious Scrupnor.

Arbican's stern tone was enough to make Scrupnor snatch his hands away and Mallory stumbled back against the wall. She had hoped the enchanter might whisk the two of them out of the counting room as quickly as he had whisked them into it; but if Arbican

had meant to cast a spell, his power once more had gone astray. In defending her, he had only drawn Scrupnor's anger upon himself.

"Who the devil are you?" shouted Scrupnor, now giving full attention to Mallory's companion. Without waiting for a reply, he began yelling for Bolt; and at the same time snatched up a pistol from the table and ordered the intruders to stand as they were. A moment later, the gamekeeper flung open the door.

"Damn you, Bolt," cried Scrupnor. "I told you, never let anyone in my counting room."

"Squire, I didn't," protested the gamekeeper, astonished at the sight of Mallory and even more bewildered by the presence of Arbican. "I don't know how these two got by. And this old crock here, I don't even know who he is."

Without lowering his pistol, Scrupnor swung to face Arbican. "What's your name? What are you up to?"

"This is Mr. Arbican," Mallory put in hastily, afraid the enchanter and his sharp tongue might worsen matters for both of them. "He's a—traveler. He's lost his way. He stopped to ask directions—"

"I'll give him directions," returned Scrupnor. "He can go to the devil, if he hasn't been there already. Traveler, is he? Where to? The gallows?"

Despite Mallory's warning tug at his robe, Arbican stepped forward, looking Scrupnor squarely between the eyes, and tartly answered:

"If your courtesy is any measure of your conduct, you'll reach that destination sooner than I."

"Hold your tongue, old weasel!" Bolt shook his fist under the enchanter's nose. "I'll take care of him for you, Squire. Gallows bird he is. You can read it in his face."

"Wait a moment, Bolt," said Scrupnor, squinting thoughtfully at Arbican. "It seems to me I recognize this fellow. Yes, it comes back to me now. I've seen him. Oh, indeed I've seen him, on the very day the dear departed was murdered."

"That's a lie!" Mallory burst out. "You couldn't. He's been in a tree—"

"A tree?" said Scrupnor. "Yes, he was. Lurking behind one, in the woods beside the highway."

The gamekeeper's jaw dropped. "The killer himself? Why, so he must be. For here he is back again after the rest of his loot."

Scrupnor nodded in growing satisfaction. "The ways of justice are strange, Bolt, very strange. But they come round, soon or late. I've searched high and low for this brute. I'd have given all I owned to the one who caught the beast. And now it turns out that I myself am the one to apprehend him; I, who suffered most from that hideous crime. There you see the hand of providence at work. Ah, Bolt, if only the dear departed could be with us at this moment, how it would warm his heart. Now fetch some rope and we'll take this villain to the notary so I can make my sworn statement. The wench must be in this, too, somehow. Otherwise, what's she doing in company with a known criminal? There's more than meets the eye; but I'll have the truth out of her, every bit of it; I'll stop at nothing less."

CHAPTER
7

Bolt hurried from the counting room. Arbican, meantime, had been studying Scrupnor with a mixture of curiosity and contempt; now he turned calmly to Mallory:

"Ordinarily, I would resent this fellow's implication that I am a robber and a murderer. In present circumstances, I think it wiser to ignore him. Come along, we have work to do."

"He'll kill you!" exclaimed Mallory. "Don't you see he's got a pistol?"

"Whatever that is," replied Arbican, unimpressed. He gave Scrupnor a cold glance. "If that implement you're waving at me has any destructive capabilities, put it away immediately."

In answer, Scrupnor muttered a curse through his teeth and leveled the weapon at Arbican's head. The enchanter shrugged:

"Very well. Since you won't lay it down, your clumsy device is now a serpent, and a very angry one."

At that, Arbican made coiling motions with his fingers. To Mallory's dismay, the firearm stayed as it was. Scrupnor laughed:

"Not only a murderer, you're a madman!"

"No!" cried Mallory. "Look, look! The snake! Crawling out the barrel!"

Startled by Mallory's warning, and without a pause for thought, Scrupnor turned the weapon to squint at the muzzle, from which no snake whatever was emerging.

Mallory's trick, however, had given her the moment she needed. Snatching up her basket, she flung it with all strength at Scrupnor's head. Taken unawares, the squire lost his balance and stumbled back on his heels. The pistol went spinning out of his hand and discharged into the air.

"Come on! Run!" Mallory urged the enchanter while Scrupnor, on hands and knees, groped for his weapon. Arbican did not move, but only stared horrified by his encounter with firearms. Mallory seized the enchanter and hauled him so quickly from the counting room that he nearly lost his footing, and hustled him along a corridor, through the first door she came to. It led to the kitchen where, at sight of intruders, the cook dropped the meat she was setting over the fire, the serving maid flung away the stack of dishes, and both began screaming at the top of their voices.

Spying an open window, Mallory pushed Arbican over the sill and sent him tumbling into the stable yard. She would have followed but the cook, regaining some of her wits, seized Mallory by the scruff of the neck; and the serving maid picked up a long-handled spoon to flail away at the struggling girl.

The pair, however, proved no match for Mallory, determined at all cost to rejoin the enchanter. Heedless of the blows, she tore loose from the hands of the cook and went pitching headlong into the yard.

She scrambled to her feet. There was no sign of the enchanter. She glanced hurriedly in all directions, at a loss where to turn. The stables were close by and she raced toward them, thinking Arbican might have hidden in one of the stalls. At the same time, waving a pitchfork, the stable boy, Wakeling, came pelting around the corner.

Mallory turned sharply aside. Wakeling, however, paid no heed to the fleeing girl. Instead, he ran to the back of the house, where he collided with the two women and Scrupnor.

"Squire, there's a great stag in the paddock," Wakeling cried. "Come and see!"

"Damn the stag!" bellowed Scrupnor, trying to disengage himself from the excited stable boy. "Where's the old man?"

"Never saw none," answered Wakeling. "But what a stag!"

"Out of my way!" roared Scrupnor, shoving the boy aside. "Find him! Stop the girl!"

By now, Mallory had reached the nearest outbuildings and headed for the stables. From the kennels she heard the frantic yelping of Scrupnor's hunting pack and she changed her course, afraid the enchanter had blundered into the dog runs.

Suddenly, from behind a shed sprang the tallest stag Mallory had ever seen. The creature bounded across her path, reared on its haunches and shook its antlered head:

"Jump! On my back!"

Dumbfounded for the instant, Mallory could only stare at the animal, who stamped impatiently:

"Do as I say! Climb on!"

Not daring to waste another moment questioning Arbican, Mallory clambered astride. Scrupnor, with Wakeling following, pounded across the stable yard but stopped short at seeing her clinging to the prancing stag.

"There he is!" cried Wakeling. "And the cook-shop girl riding him! Now that's a sight for you, Squire!"

Sharing none of the stable boy's wonder, Scrupnor brought up his pistol and pulled the trigger. In his rage, however, he had forgotten to reload and the hammer snapped on an empty chamber. With a curse, Scrupnor flung away the useless firearm, snatched the pitchfork from the astonished Wakeling, and heaved it straight at Mallory.

The stag wheeled, and the pitchfork, nearly skewering its target, clattered to the dust. The huge animal then lowered its head and bounded for Scrupnor. Seeing the sharp antlers driving toward him, Scrupnor threw himself to the ground, yelling in terror. The stag, veering at the last moment, sped across the yard and into the pasture. Clearing the fence in one leap, it streaked for the woods.

Mallory, heart in her mouth, clamped arms and legs around the stag as it crashed through the underbrush,

plunged into a thicket, and at all speed pressed deeper into the tangle of branches and vines.

Only when the Holdings were far behind them did the stag halt and let Mallory slide off. Still breathless and shaken by their narrow escape, and amazed at Arbican's new transformation, Mallory threw her arms around the animal's neck.

"You saved us! Your power's come back. That's wonderful!"

The stag snorted. "Wonderful! I meant to change myself into a horse."

"You came close," Mallory said. "You had most of it right: four legs, hooves—"

"And these ridiculous branches growing out of my head. Good luck I didn't turn into a cow. No, I still don't have the hang of it. My power isn't working well at all. I certainly didn't foresee appearing under the very nose of your squire. You did better than I," the enchanter admitted. "Very clever. I wish I had thought of it. If you hadn't tricked him so neatly, there's no telling what he might have done."

"I know what he'd have done," said Mallory. "He'd have shot you."

"No doubt. Yes, the pistol, that infernal machine. Leave it to you mortals to turn a harmless concoction to some nasty purpose."

"Gunpowder? You know about that?"

"If that's what you call it, of course I do. All of us enchanters did. A little pinch here and there, sprinkled over a fire—a childish amusement. But we had better sense than to give you humans the secret. Apparently you learned it for yourselves. Well, you're ingenious, I'll say that much. Which, alas, is not quite the same as intelligent. Why that crude oaf insisted I had anything to do with some sordid local crime is altogether beyond me. From the very look of him, I should say it was more his sort of thing than mine."

"He lied," agreed Mallory, "and I can guess why." She quickly explained what had happened to Sorrel, adding: "For all his tears about avenging his dear departed master, he's never found the one who did it."

"And seizes on me as a convenient scapegoat," put in Arbican. "Yes, if I judge him rightly, that's how his mind would work. Crude, but unfortunately not unusual, even in my day."

"Emmet and some others in the village think it was Scrupnor himself," Mallory said, "and after what happened now, so do I. But no one can prove it, I certainly can't. If you'd given me my wishes, I know how I'd use one of them."

"Admirable," replied the enchanter. "But if you really mean that, I'm sure you can manage it yourself. You're a brave girl, and a good-hearted one. That should be enough magic for anybody."

The stag's mouth shut abruptly, in a manner exactly like Arbican's, as the enchanter considered the matter closed. His words, however, had given Mallory neither confidence nor comfort. At the same time, to her dismay, she heard the baying of hounds. Scrupnor had loosed his hunting pack.

The stag, too, heard the dogs and jumped to its feet.

"Climb on. They're far behind us. I can outrun them easily."

"If they catch your scent," warned Mallory, "they'll

stay on your trail. Can't you change yourself back again?"

"If I could," returned Arbican, "don't you think I would? These antlers are giving me a headache. I don't see how stags put up with them. Habit, I suppose. Well, come on, come on, stop chattering."

"Where shall we go?" asked Mallory, once again clambering to the stag's back.

"To the oak. A boat is still my best chance of reaching Vale Innis. How I shall build one with these hooves instead of hands, I have no idea. What about those tools?"

"I'll try to get them for you," said Mallory as the stag trotted swiftly through the deepening shadows. "It won't be easy. Scrupnor's bound to raise a hue and cry. He'll set the whole village after you. And me, too, for that matter. I don't know what to do."

"You don't have much choice," Arbican replied. "You can help me if you want, or we can part company here and now."

"Of course I want to help you," answered Mallory. Then she added painfully, "Once you're on your way to Vale Innis, I don't know what I'll do. If I go back to the village, Scrupnor's likely to have me in prison, or worse. Even if he doesn't, I hate to think what Mrs. Parsel will do to me."

"Then it's still simpler," the enchanter said. "Either you go back to the village and take your chances, or you don't. If you don't go back, then obviously you must go somewhere else. Don't complain. I have less choice than you. Either I find my way to Vale Innis or I die here."

76

"How can you be so coldblooded about it?" Mallory burst out. She had been hoping for more comfort, or at least sympathy from Arbican. "Doesn't anything matter to you? Don't you even care what happens to you?"

"Whether I care or not has nothing to do with the facts of the matter. I told you before: I create illusions, I don't mistake them for the way things are."

"If only you'd given me my wishes when I asked you," Mallory said, half angrily. "I could have helped both of us."

"Wishes again!" the stag snorted. "Next, you'll be at me again to take you to Vale Innis."

"I will not!" cried Mallory. "I wouldn't go there even if you begged me! You're selfish, heartless, bad-tempered—the whole world could tumble down, for all the difference it makes to you. If that's the way enchanters are, I'd rather stay here. I don't care about your wishes, either," she sobbed, too exhausted to keep back her tears. "I don't want them and I don't need them. I'll look after myself."

"At last you're showing some sense," Arbican calmly replied, halting as Mallory jumped from his back. "A little rest and you won't be so edgy. I find myself somewhat weary in the legs; disappointing, as I expected rather more vigor from a stag. There's no use going further tonight. I intend to have a nap. I suggest you do the same."

Mallory did not answer. She had turned away from the enchanter, and when at last she ventured a glance over her shoulder she saw the stag had folded his legs on the ground and shut his eyes. The rising moon turned the great antlers to silver; the animal's powerful neck and haunches were dappled in the pale light washing over them. Even if she had not known the stag's shape held Arbican within it, she would have sensed nonetheless a magical creature.

But it was a magic, she realized, she could never share. Drudging for Mrs. Parsel, she had dreamed of wishes coming true. Arbican had made it clear that her hopes were vain. "I was happier before I met a real enchanter," Mallory admitted to herself. "Then, at least, I could make believe something marvelous would happen to me. I can't even do that any more."

She crouched on the turf and hunched down amid the drift of fallen leaves. The dogs had stopped baying, but she was sure Scrupnor had not given up the hunt. She tried to force herself to stay awake; but her weariness overcame her fears, and her eyes closed as she huddled deeper into the leaves.

She awoke with a start. Something was nudging her shoulder. The moon had vanished in a mottled sky. Arbican's voice was urging her to get up. Still drowsy, she raised her head. Then she clapped a hand over her mouth.

Two beady eyes were squinting at her from the pink, plump-cheeked face of a half-grown pig.

CHAPTER
8

 "Yes, it's me," Arbican grunted angrily. "It's happened again. A goose could have served some purpose. A stag at least has bearing and dignity. But a common swine?"

The pig sank back and waved its forefeet in the air. Its jowls shook and the sleek body swelled with indignation. Despite her miseries, and Arbican's own plight, Mallory could scarcely keep herself from laughing; had she not been certain that the enchanter would be mortally insulted, she would have reached out and patted the fat, round cheeks.

"If it makes you feel any better," Mallory said, "you're very handsome. You're the most beautiful pig I've ever seen."

"What's that to do with anything?" snorted Arbican. "Don't you understand? I still can't get my powers back in hand. Who knows what next? A donkey? A goat? I might as well spend my life in a barnyard. Oh, they'll snicker over this in Vale Innis—if I ever get there. Pig, indeed! A laughingstock! An ignominious transmogrification!"

"You might have changed your shape," said Mallory, "but that's no reason to change your plan. We'll go back to your tree, just as you meant to do. You'll have your boat, if I have to put together every stick of it myself."

By way of thanks, the pig merely grunted. Disregarding Arbican's brusque manner, Mallory stood, shook the leaves and twigs from her dress, and beckoned for him to follow. Muttering to himself, the pig trotted after her as she set off in what she hoped was the shortest path to the oak. However, she had scarcely taken three paces when she cried out in alarm.

In the bushes, so close she could almost have touched him, stood a lanky, red-faced young farmer, frozen in his tracks. He had dropped the bundle of firewood he had been gathering; the ax had slipped from his hands; his jaw hung slack with astonishment. At first, Mallory feared the intruder had come from the Holdings; now she saw it was Burdick, the son of Farmer Tench. There was no doubt that Burdick recognized her, too. But how long he had been watching, and what he had seen or heard, Mallory could not guess. Deciding her only choice was to brazen it out, Mallory drew herself up, and declared:

"Shame on you, standing there ogling people! Be off or I'll tell your father."

Mallory's outburst shook Burdick into movement.

He slowly raised his arm and pointed a finger at the enchanter.

"That," said Burdick, as if he had pondered the matter from all sides and made up his mind past any question, "that's a pig."

"Of course it's a pig," retorted Mallory. "What did you think it was?"

"And you," Burdick went on, turning his gaze and his finger toward Mallory, "you were talking to it."

"Why shouldn't I?" demanded Mallory. "Do you never talk to your cow when you milk her? I always talk to my pig. He keeps me company and he has better manners than somebody who hides in the bushes, eavesdropping on other folk."

"Talk to him as you like," replied Burdick. "But here's the nub of it: that pig was answering."

Mallory's heart sank as she realized Burdick had indeed overheard their conversation. Nevertheless, looking squarely at him, she insisted:

"That's ridiculous. There's no such thing as a talking pig."

Burdick nodded. "None I ever met before. But my old dad told me once he heard a bird with a voice clear as a man. A greeny-yellowy creature with a beak all hooked out of shape and out of nature; but it talked as clever as a schoolmaster."

"That's a poll-parrot," said Mallory. "They're supposed to talk; everybody knows that."

"Right!" exclaimed Burdick, his face lighting up. "So this will be a poll-piggy!"

"No!" cried Mallory. "It's no kind of pig at all."

"If it isn't," replied Burdick, "then it's the ugliest, nakedest baby I've ever seen." He squatted in front of Arbican and peered into the bristly face. Arbican stared back with ill-concealed annoyance; then, snorting irritably, turned away. Burdick, however, determined to study this remarkable animal at closer range, seized the plump cheeks in both hands.

"Stop that immediately," snapped Arbican, pulling his head free of Burdick's grip. "I may have no say about my shape, but I'm not required to be pinched and prodded by some ignorant rustic who calls me ugly, into the bargain!"

Mallory threw her hands up in despair. Her best hope had been somehow to convince the stubborn Burdick to disbelieve his own ears. Arbican's bad temper and wounded vanity had wrecked any chance of that; all the more since the enchanter kept on with his tongue lashing, beyond the possibility of anyone's mistaking his power of speech.

Burdick, instead of taking offense, only seemed immensely pleased at finding his judgment so fully borne out. He nodded his head, as though he had seen dozens of such creatures and was deeply knowledgeable in all their ways:

"Yes, that's one of them poll-piggies, all right. Where'd you get him?"

"Nowhere," Mallory answered hastily. "I mean, I found him in the woods." She said no more, for her one wish was to get Arbican as far as she could from Burdick, before the enchanter's tongue brought him worse grief. But the farmer was not to be put off:

"He must be worth a little something, eh? My old

dad says he paid threepence to hear that poll-parrot. Why, folks should give half a crown to hear this fellow, for he's ten times the size of a bird. Whoever owned him could make a fortune on market days, just showing him off."

"Half a crown, indeed!" muttered Arbican. "Whatever that may be worth, it's hardly ample compensation. Merciful moon, to be made a spectacle for a crowd of yokels!"

"They'd come for miles to hear him," Burdick went on. "From as far as Castleton." He narrowed his eyes at Mallory. "What will you take for him?"

"He's not for sale. I told you he isn't that kind of pig."

"That's a shame and a waste," replied Burdick. "To keep a curiosity like him and not turn some profit from it? A man would have to be a born fool if he let a prize like that go by."

Mallory saw a crafty look come into Burdick's face. She moved closer to Arbican, meaning to pick him up and be gone before Burdick could think any further on the matter. The farmer, however, was quicker on his feet than Mallory had expected. He darted past her, snatched Arbican by the hind trotters, tucked him firmly under his arm, and plunged through the bushes.

Shouting for him to stop, Mallory raced after the fleeing Burdick. Even with her strong legs and all the speed she could muster, she could not overtake the farmer, who rapidly outdistanced her and vanished into the woods. She could heard the pig squealing and bawling at the top of its voice. Following the cries, she soon reached the edge of a clearing, where she caught sight

of Burdick, with Arbican kicking and sputtering under his arm, loping with great strides across a plowed field.

Burdick was racing to the farmhouse that lay a short way ahead. Doubling her efforts, Mallory stumbled over the furrows, leaped a wall of stones, sped past the outbuildings and halted near the barn. Arbican's outcries had ceased, and she glanced around, uncertain where Burdick had taken him. In another moment, she heard voices, ran toward them, and found herself in a rutted yard near the stock pens.

There, Burdick was shouting excitedly at the burly, gray-headed Farmer Tench, who was studying the pig with keen interest, weighing the struggling animal with his eyes, and giving much less attention to his son, frantically jigging up and down.

"You see what I brought you, old dad?" Burdick cried. "You see this fellow here? You know what he is?"

The elder Tench leaned on his rake, thoughtfully worked his jaws for several moments, then curtly nodded:

"Pork."

At this, his offspring chuckled and wrinkled his face into a knowing grin. "There's some as might say that."

"I say it," replied Farmer Tench. Finishing his silent calculations, and appearing highly satisfied with them, he cocked a thumb toward the pen:

"In there with him. Light a fire under the scalding vat and I'll sharpen my sticker."

CHAPTER
9

 At that, Burdick hooted gleefully, as if he had succeeded in playing an enormous joke on his elder. "Stick him? You'll stick away a fortune! He's better than any pork you've ever seen, old dad. You'll be ever grateful I found him."

"You didn't find him!" cried Mallory, who by this time had run to join the two farmers. "You stole him!"

She would have tried then and there to snatch Arbican from Burdick; but the latter spun away to take refuge behind the solid bulk of his parent:

"Don't you listen to her, old dad! He's a stray. He's as much mine as hers. More, as he was closer to our land."

Tench eyed Mallory as he had previously eyed the pig. "What are you doing out of the cook-shop? Does Parsel know what you're up to?"

"I was tending my pig—" Mallory began.

"Parsel don't keep pigs," answered Tench. "So he can't be yours."

"I found him in the woods. He belongs to me and I want him back."

"Hold on there," said Tench, fending off Mallory, who was still trying to come to grips with his son. "You tell me what you were doing in these parts to begin with."

"That's right, old dad," put in Burdick. "She's got no business around here, coming to take our fortune away from us."

"Stop rattling, boy," commanded Tench. "I'll get to the bottom of this. She might have a claim and she might not."

"Don't you listen to her, whatever she says," cried Burdick. "She'll do us out of bushels of gold! Don't you know what I've got here? It's a poll-piggy!"

Tench frowned at his son, who hurried on:

"You remember that green bird you told about? That talked as clear as a man? Well, this one's the same."

"Boy," said Tench, "if you think this pig's a green bird, you go straight away and cool your head under the pump. You tell me: Do you see one feather on him?"

"No, no!" protested Burdick. "I mean he talks. Talks, do you hear? Like you and me. I caught a treasure for us!"

"You lock that pig in the pen," said Farmer Tench. "Then get yourself to bed and I'll give you a fluxion. You caught a brain fever, that's what you caught."

"I tell you this poll-piggy talks," Burdick insisted,

as he lifted Arbican over the wooden fence and dropped him into the muddy enclosure. "You should've heard him when I was bringing him here. He called me every spiteful name he could think of."

"So he should," replied Tench. "And did he call you a jackass for thinking a swine can talk?"

"You just listen to him," declared Burdick, hauling his father closer to the railing. Mallory at the same time clambered hastily into the pen, where she knelt beside Arbican and threw her arms protectively around his neck. "Go on, old dad, have a word with him. You'll see how he answers back. He'll make your ears burn."

Tench hesitated and shook his head. Burdick, however, so pushed and prodded him that he grudgingly cleared his throat, and loudly demanded:

"Now, pig, speak up."

Mallory held her breath, expecting Arbican would be more than willing to give Farmer Tench a piece of his mind. Instead, to Mallory's relief, the enchanter wisely held his tongue and merely stared wordlessly at his captors.

Tench turned angrily to his son. "That's what you're up to, eh? One of your pranks? To have me make a fool of myself?"

"Give him a chance, old dad," said Burdick. "You're too quick with him. He's a skittish creature. You've put him off, going at him so short." With that, Burdick doffed his hat, bent down, and went on in a cajoling voice:

"How do you do, sir? You're looking well, Master Porker. That's a fine curly tail you have, sir. Now, I don't hold it against you, what you said to me. We're friends, us two. We'll both have our fortunes made. On my word, you'll be well looked after. A pail of swill every day, that's what you'd like, eh? Now, what do you say to that?"

In reply, the pig turned away and began rooting among the clods in the pen. Tench flung down his rake, seized his son by the scruff of his neck, and hauled him to his feet:

"Leave off! You've more to do than pass the time of day with a pig."

Seeing his prize betraying him, and the fortune in danger of vanishing before it had even come into his hands, Burdick shook his fist at Mallory:

"That's your fault! You're egging him on to hold his tongue. You make him speak up like he did before."

"I told you pigs don't talk," Mallory flung back.

"I heard what I heard. Unless you were tricking me some way. Enticing me to think he was a true poll-piggy, and then fob off any sort of dumb swine!"

"I didn't ask you to steal him," returned Mallory, hoping Arbican's refusal to speak had convinced the Tenches there was no profit in keeping him. She was about to open the gate of the pen while Burdick continued to upbraid her for cheating him. Farmer Tench, who had gone off to the shed, now reappeared.

"You do as I say," he told his son. "You set that scalding vat bubbling."

"What for?" cried Mallory, horrified to see a long, thin-bladed knife in the farmer's hand. "You can't mean to butcher him!"

Tench stared at her, puzzled. "That I do," he said. "I'll have some use out of this fellow. We don't get meat like this from one month to the next."

"Stay away!" cried Mallory, running to the side of Arbican. "Don't you touch him!"

"Now, lass," replied the farmer in a soothing voice, "no cause to take on like that. I'll set matters right with Parsel. You'll have a nice bit of fresh ham to take back to him; some chops, too. That's a fair share, as I have all the work to do."

Burdick clapped his hands. "Hear that, you worthless poll-piggy? You had your chance. Now it's the pork barrel for you!"

Mallory caught up the pig in her arms. "Tell them who you are," she whispered in his ear. "Try to turn into something else! Anything! They're going to slaughter you!"

Arbican only snuffled; and now it was Mallory's turn to beg him to speak. Burdick, meantime, whooped and shouted mockingly:

"Souse and sausage! Bacon and lard! Serves you right! Now you'll squeal a tasty tune!"

In spite of Mallory's urging, Arbican voiced no more than a desperate grunting. His plump cheeks had gone red with his efforts and, in growing terror, Mallory realized his powers had once more failed him.

Farmer Tench, with Burdick following eagerly, strode into the pen. From his smock, he pulled out a length of cord as he told Mallory:

"That's right, you hold him fast. I'll tie up his trotters. Then let him kick all he wants."

90

"No!" cried Mallory. "He's not a pig!"

Tench squinted at her and sadly shook his head. "I thought my boy was addled. Poor thing, you're worse off than he is. Look there at that snout. Pure pig, if ever I've seen one. Look there at that twisty tail. Now, if he's not a pig true as all nature, you tell me what he is."

"An enchanter!" blurted Mallory, seeing only disaster in keeping Arbican's identity a secret. "He's a wizard. He changed into a pig and now he can't change back. Before, he was a stag—"

"Sure he was," replied Tench, agreeably. "Or a fox, a badger, whatever suits your fancy. Wizard, you say? Then, so he is; and we'll have wizard for supper, smoked and salted."

"You can't kill him," insisted Mallory. "That's murder!"

"That's meat!" said the farmer, brandishing his knife. "Witless or no, you're not keeping food off my table. Now, do as I say, girl, or I swear I'll carve him where he is."

Mallory tightened her hold on Arbican, whose frantic squealing convinced her all the more that his power of speech had vanished. However, by no means had he lost his understanding, for the look in his eyes told her he knew very well what the farmer intended.

"Carve him?" cried Mallory. "You'll have to carve me, first!"

His face reddening, Tench shook the knife under Mallory's nose. "Is that how Parsel brought you up? To back-talk your elders? Rub me the wrong way and you'll see what you get."

"That's right, old dad," shouted Burdick. "You tell

her! She did us out of our fortune, she's not going to do us out of our bacon!"

Tench hesitated, not really willing to carry out his threat; but uncertain how to deal with Mallory, who had stubbornly planted her feet and never budged an inch from where she stood. Seeing his father's puzzled frown, Burdick snatched the knife away and with a bloodcurdling yell, made as if to plunge it into Mallory's throat.

The blade stopped a hair's breadth from its mark, but it was all Mallory could do to keep herself from flinching. Trembling though she was, she looked Burdick boldly in the eyes, hoping her fear showed less than her determination.

"Stop it!" ordered Tench. "Fools, both of you!" He beckoned to his son. "Put down that sticker. Give me a hand before you do harm past mending."

Dropping the knife, Burdick joined his father, who now tried by sheer force to pull the squealing pig from Mallory's grasp. Though Arbican kicked sharply, and Mallory did her best to break free, she was no match for the two farmers. Burdick pummeled and buffeted her, Tench tugged with all his might at the enchanter; until at last Mallory's strength gave way and she fell, sobbing with anger, to the muddy ground.

"You got him, old dad!" Whooping triumphantly, Burdick ran from the pen and started for the shed. Mallory scrambled to her feet and threw herself upon Farmer Tench. Taken unawares by this new assault, Tench stumbled to his knees and flung out a hand to break his fall. The pig wriggled loose and darted through the gate.

Tench bawled for his son to head off the fleeing animal, who scurried with all the speed of its flying trotters out of the yard and across the field.

Mallory would have followed; but, as she raced from the enclosure, a horse-drawn wagon lumbered into the farmyard. Before she could spring aside, the driver jumped down and blocked her way.

"Never mind the girl!" shouted Farmer Tench. "Get the pig!"

The wagon driver paid no attention to the farmer's yelling. Instead, blinking in astonishment, he caught Mallory by the arm.

"What have you done?" cried Mr. Parsel. "Squire's got all the village looking for you!"

CHAPTER 10

The face of the would-be innkeeper puckered and he looked as unhappily surprised to see Mallory as she to see him.

"Oh, Mallie," cried Mr. Parsel. "Where have you been? What have you done? Mrs. P.'s nearly had a seizure, she's that upset. Squire's put up a reward for you, like a common criminal."

"I've done nothing but help an—an old man," Mallory returned. "That's no crime, whatever Scrupnor says."

"Old man? Why, he's the brute who did away with poor Sorrel. Squire caught him dead to rights—and you along with him. Oh, poor girl, what have you got yourself into? Good thing I came to buy vegetables from Tench. Who knows what would happen if someone else found you!"

From Mr. Parsel's expression, Mallory judged he was

desperately wishing he had never found her in the first place. He squeezed his eyes tightly shut, as though fervently hoping that when he opened them again, Mallory would have disappeared.

"I won't go back to the village," Mallory declared. "My friend's in worse trouble than I am. I have to find him. Scrupnor's a liar. He's blaming Arbican for something he didn't do."

"Who's Arbican?" Mr. Parsel hastily added, "No, no, don't tell me. I don't want to know. Things are in enough of a stew. If you don't come back, you'll make matters worse."

"How could I do that?" Mallory replied bitterly. She braced herself, ready to fend off any attempt by Mr. Parsel to force her into the wagon. Mr. Parsel, however, showed no sign of wanting to pit his strength against Mallory's determination, but only looked all the more woebegone.

"Well, then," said Mr. Parsel, "what shall you do?" He glanced uneasily behind him, as if he were afraid Scrupnor might overhear him or, worse, Mrs. Parsel, and added in a low voice:

"Mallie, you're not a wicked girl, whatever anyone says. If there's a way to help you—"

By now, having given up any hope of recapturing the pig, Farmer Tench and his son came to join Mr. Parsel. While Burdick glared at Mallory, Tench burst out angrily:

"Parsel, your wench cost me some fine ham and pork chops—and you might have had a share of them, too. My boy found her with a pig on my land. Stolen, for all I know; but she had no business with it in the first place.

If it hadn't been for her stubbornness, I'd have him curing in the smokehouse this very moment."

"That's right, old dad," Burdick put in. "And she tried to make fools of us with a poll-piggy that couldn't even speak his own name."

"Don't tell me anything about stolen pigs," said Mr. Parsel. "I don't want to know about that, either."

"Well, you'll want to know she needs a good whipping," Tench said, "and I mean to give her one."

As the farmer made to unbuckle his belt, Mr. Parsel choked, gulped, and at last managed to declare with uncustomary boldness:

"No, you won't. If she's to be punished, I'll see to that myself." At the same time, he took Mallory's arm and drew her to the wagon. Taken aback by Mr. Parsel's show of authority, Tench spat and grumbled, but did nothing to carry out his threat.

For her part, Mallory was only too glad for any means that would get her away from Tench and Burdick. She jumped quickly to the seat beside Mr. Parsel, who slapped the reins against the horse's flanks and sent the wagon creaking out of the farmyard.

"If you want to help me," said Mallory, once they were out of sight, "you can drive me fast as you can to the edge of that field."

As the wagon jolted along the rutted lane, Mallory peered past the hedgerows, hoping to catch some glimpse of Arbican.

"What are you looking for?" Mr. Parsel asked, urging the horse to a brisker pace.

"My friend," Mallory answered. "He ran into the woods. He may be looking for me, too."

"The murderer?" Mr. Parsel's cheeks paled, and he seemed ready to halt the wagon and take to his heels.

"I told you he's done no harm," said Mallory. "If we find him, you'll see for yourself."

At the prospect of coming face to face with a wanted fugitive, Mr. Parsel trembled violently. "No, no thank you," he said hastily. "I want nothing to do with that fellow."

He sighed miserably. "Squire's in such a state, he'd likely take my inn away, hypothecation and all, if he thought I had hands on you and didn't bring you to him."

He frowned, chewed his lip, and looked all the more distressed as he went on:

"Now, as to where I found you—if the question ever comes up, as I hope it doesn't, but if, as you might say, it arises, ah, there's no need to put Farmer Tench into it. To go at it another way, he should be kept out of it. Altogether out of it. In other words, in a manner of speaking, you weren't there. And neither was I."

"If you're ashamed to admit you helped me—" began Mallory.

"Well, well, you see—it's more a matter of my hypothecation. A question of vegetables, do you see? Vegetables, here, is the case in point."

Mallory, straining her eyes for a sign of the enchanter, was in no mood to discuss this mixture of hypothecation and vegetables. However, as she said nothing, Mr. Parsel's discomfort sharpened:

"Well, you see, in terms of my agreement, I'm to buy my victualization from Squire's tenants. Now, Farmer Tench doesn't stand that way with Squire, exactly. That is, he's not a tenant. On the other hand, his prices are very reasonable. On still the other hand, Squire's aren't reasonable. The fact of the matter, he's gone and raised them.

"I'm afraid," Mr. Parsel gloomily continued, "my hypothecation is going to pinch. If I buy only from Squire's tenants, I'll pay too dear to make a profit. Now, Mrs. P.—that woman's mind is quick as a trap—she put it into my head, in the way of suggesting the possibility, without Squire having to know about it, to buy my victualization from the freeholders on more favorizing terms. To put a fine point to it: on the cheap."

"It won't do you any good," answered Mallory. "Not for long. What happens when Scrupnor adds up his tenants' accounts and sees you've bought nothing?"

Mr. Parsel's face went chalky. "Eh, so he will. I never thought of that. Nor did Mrs. P. Ah, Mallie, no disrespect to Squire, you understand, but I'm afraid he's got me well skewered. My fortune? That hypothecation's my ruin!"

Mr. Parsel seemed on the verge of tears. For the first time in all the years Mallory had drudged for her benefactors, it occurred to her that Mr. Parsel might have been as unhappy as she was. Now, between the two of them, she wondered which was the worse off. Before she could reply, as Mr. Parsel once more began moaning over his hypothecation, Mallory believed she glimpsed a pale flicker of movement through the hedgerows further down the lane.

"Hurry," she urged Mr. Parsel. "That might be the pig."

"Pig? I thought you were after your friend—"

"It's the same—oh, never mind, only hurry!"

Doing as she urged, Mr. Parsel vigorously slapped the reins. The startled horse plunged forward, the wagon lurched from side to side. Trying to control his animal and his vehicle, Mr. Parsel now pulled up so sharply that the horse stopped in its tracks and the wagon came to such a sudden halt that Mallory went pitching headlong over the side, Mr. Parsel along with her.

Half-stunned, Mallory picked herself up, impatient to set off again. Mr. Parsel was still sprawled in the middle of the road. She ran to help him, then gasped in alarm. His cheeks and brow had gone ashen, he lay awkward and motionless.

As Mallory tried to raise him and prop him against a wagon wheel, she saw that a large lump was beginning to swell where Mr. Parsel had struck his head in falling. Alive though he was, she could not guess how much harm the blow had done. She loosened his collar and chafed his wrists, but none of her efforts roused him.

She glanced anxiously down the lane and across the fields. If indeed it was Arbican she had seen, there was no longer any sign of him. Without knowing which direction the enchanter might take, she realized her only course was to strike across the fields and hope somehow to run into him. However, much as she urged herself to let the prostrate Mr. Parsel come to his own senses and make the best of his way home, she could not bring herself to do it. As often as she started off, as often she came back, furious beyond reason at the would-be innkeeper, as if being knocked on the head were his fault; and furious at herself for being unable to leave him by the roadside.

At last she decided, whatever the cost in time and risk, to cart him to the Tench farm. Though Mr. Parsel was a mere wisp in comparison with the proportions of his wife, he was nevertheless heavier than Mallory had supposed; only with difficulty was she able to hoist him to the back of the wagon. Worse, she quickly discovered that turning the vehicle in the narrow lane was an even harder task. The horse balked and shied away from her, quite aware that Mallory was not its customary driver.

No sooner had she managed to calm the animal than the wagon foundered in a deep rut at the edge of the road; while the horse pulled as willingly as it could, Mallory pushed and heaved, set her shoulder against the rear wheel, and gripped the spokes with her rapidly blistering fingers. The wagon, tilting alarmingly, finally rolled free onto the road again.

During all this, Mr. Parsel had not stirred; but as Mallory, shaking from her efforts, was about to climb to the seat, she heard a feeble moaning. Mr. Parsel had half-opened his eyes.

"I'm driving you to Farmer Tench," Mallory said, as Mr. Parsel cautiously ventured to sit up. "You can stay there until you feel better. Or you can ask his boy to take you the rest of the way to the village."

Mr. Parsel, fingering the black and blue swelling at the side of his head, turned a grateful glance on Mallory. "You could have been long gone," he murmured, "and taken wagon and all if you'd wanted. Oh, Mallie, do

come home with me. I don't care if Squire finds out I was buying victuals on the sly; I'll tell him how well you behaved, that's bound to count in your favor. He'll deal with you fairly."

"Yes," Mallory answered. "As fairly as he dealt with you. He knows perfectly well Arbican's no criminal and neither am I. If anything, Scrupnor himself did away with Squire Sorrel."

"Good heavens," replied Mr. Parsel, "what a thing to say about a man of progress and vision. True, my hypothecation cuts rather deeper than I reckoned. But business is one thing, foul play another."

Mallory did not answer, more anxious to be unburdened of Mr. Parsel than to discuss her suspicions with him. The Tench farm should be close by, and she wondered if Mr. Parsel might now be recovered enough to go the rest of the way alone.

Suddenly, she pulled back on the reins. A little distance ahead, she caught sight of Bolt, on horseback; afoot beside him were one of the grooms from the Holdings and the stable boy, Wakeling. While Mr. Parsel peered over the side of the wagon, cradling his head with one hand and with the other shading his eyes to see what was amiss, Mallory sprang down, ready to take to her heels.

A moment later, she halted. With Bolt and the others, hands roped behind him, was Arbican.

 The gamekeeper saw Mallory at the same instant and kicked his horse to a gallop. With Arbican a prisoner, Mallory gave up any thought of escape. Instead of heading for the cover of the woods, she ran straight to the enchanter and threw her arms around him, stammering questions. Horn, the groom, seized her and pulled her away. Bolt, having immediately turned his mount after her, jumped from the saddle.

"Hold fast, Horn," he called. "She's tricky as Old Scratch here. Wakeling, get hold of her arms. Mind what you're about. The wench kicks worse than donkeys."

The gamekeeper at the same time pulled a length of cord from his jacket and hastily lashed Mallory's wrists. Her struggles, however, were not to break free but to stay close to the captive enchanter. Arbican's face was haggard, his cheeks a sickly gray, and his beard hung limp. At first sight of Mallory, he had brightened; but now he eyed her with deliberate severity. In spite of his bedraggled appearance, his voice and words were tart as ever:

"I gave you credit for better sense. By the vernal equinox, girl, you could have outrun these idiots. You can't help me this way, and you certainly can't do yourself any good."

Mallory paid no attention to the enchanter's pretended irritation. He looked ill and exhausted and she feared his time was growing dangerously short. "Scrupnor can't do anything to either of us," she said with more assurance than she felt.

"Oh, can't he?" put in Bolt, overhearing their exchange. "He'll have this old lag hanged for murder, that's one thing. And for you helping him escape, who knows what he'll do? You're for prison, at the least of it." Bolt grinned at her and clamped her cheeks between his fingers. "Unless I was to tell him how repentent and agreeable you are."

Mallory twisted her head from his grip and spat at him. Cursing, Bolt struck her across the face with a blow that nearly sent her spinning to the ground. Arbican, weak though he was, lunged at the gamekeeper, only to be held back by Horn.

Mr. Parsel, meanwhile, had gathered enough strength to draw up his wagon amid the captors and their prisoners. Shakily, still unsteady on his legs, he tried to clamber down, at the same time calling out:

"Here, Bolt, none of that! She's my servant and she's still in my charge."

Bolt strode up to him and seized him by the jacket front. "Charge your nose to keep out of this, you milk-pudding. Afraid you'll be done out of the reward? Well, you make your claim to Squire after we get them to the Holdings."

With Bolt's jaw thrusting at his face, Mr. Parsel shrank back and murmured:

"Now, now, Mr. Bolt, no cause for quarrel. She did me a good turn. I shouldn't want to see her abused."

"She won't be." Bolt laughed scornfully. "I'll care for those two like tender babes. They're money in pocket, especially Old Nick here. He's mine, that one. Sorry sight he is, but he's worth his weight in gold."

"It wasn't only you that found him," protested Horn. "I collared him, didn't I? I have a share coming to me."

Bolt loosened his hold on Mr. Parsel's jacket and faced the groom:

"What's that, you muckraker? I say I saw him first, and that's what counts. You'll get your part of him. I'll be openhanded with you for your help, such as it was. I won't stint. Only you try telling a tale different from mine, I won't stint, either." Bolt put a hand to the musket slung at his saddle bow and glared ferociously at the groom, who dropped his eyes and turned away, muttering under his breath.

Mallory, during this, had drawn closer to Arbican. "I was looking for you," she whispered. "You were better off being a pig. Couldn't you have stayed that way?"

Arbican shook his head. "Something was going wrong when I lost my voice. Since I didn't know what might happen next, it seemed wise to depart as rapidly as possible. Ham and bacon, indeed! If it hadn't been for you, no doubt I'd be curing in a rustic smokehouse. My magic failed me. Fortunately, yours didn't."

"Mine?" said Mallory. "I have no magic. I wish I did. I'd have given anything in the world if I could have snapped my fingers and turned us both invisible. Or sent us flying off on a broomstick."

"Broomstick?" replied Arbican. "That sounds like another of your irrelevant appurtenances. Me, straddle a broomstick? I'd feel like an utter idiot. No, I was not referring to my variety of magic, but yours, call it what you will. You could have had your throat cut. You weren't bluffing! Very brave; though not without an element of foolhardiness."

The enchanter's usually stern glance had softened and it seemed to Mallory that he was watching her with an affection and admiration he had not shown before. Almost immediately, however, Arbican assumed his familiar scowl as he went on:

"In any case, I couldn't have stayed a pig even if I'd wanted. I couldn't hold the shape. After a time, it slipped away and there I was, back to myself again. I thought if I could change into a bird, I could find you more easily. That's what I was trying to do when that oaf took me by surprise. Too bad. Another minute or so and I might have done it. I could almost feel the pin-feathers sprouting."

Arbican said no more, for the stable boy, Wakeling, had sidled up to Mallory.

"Who's the old codger?" Wakeling asked out of the corner of his mouth, eyeing Arbican with frank curiosity. "How did you ever come to tangle with him?

107

He's an odd one, for sure. You should have seen him when Horn and I came up on him. Standing on a stump, he was, flapping his arms like he was about to fly off at any moment. Squire says he's a vicious mad dog, but if you ask me—" At that, Wakeling tapped his forehead with a finger.

"Listen to me," Mallory whispered, "he's done no harm to anyone. Help us get free. He's an enchanter, a wizard—"

"One of them conjurers?" replied Wakeling. "Like at Castleton Fair? Take a penny out of your nose quick as winking! I saw one make a fellow's watch disappear —and never brought it back again, though. Eh, imagine that, an old Hocus-Pocus!"

"He's not a conjurer," Mallory tried to explain. But Wakeling, more fascinated than ever, stared closer at Arbican.

"Is that so, Hocus?" the stable boy asked. "You can do all such tricks? And here you are, trussed like a prize turkey?"

Before Mallory could make a further plea, Bolt left off his browbeating of the groom and shouted for the prisoners to be put into Mr. Parsel's wagon.

"You come along, Hocus," Wakeling said. "You too, Mallie. I'm sorry for you, but what's to be done? If I tried to set you loose, Bolt he'd have my hide and Squire the rest of me."

"Get a move on," called Bolt, mounting his horse. "I don't mean to be soaked to the skin while you stand there maundering."

The sky, in fact, had begun turning the same color as Mr. Parsel's bruise, and Mallory heard the first mutterings of thunder. Wakeling boosted Arbican into the wagon but before Mallory could follow the enchanter, Mr. Parsel held her back and put a hand almost shyly on her arm.

"It's a shame things have come to such a pass," he murmured, "as knotted up as me and my hypothecation. But you'll find some way, if you look—"

"Have done, damn you!" cried Bolt, motioning for Mr. Parsel to set off, as Wakeling hopped into the back with the two prisoners. On the wagon seat, however, Mr. Parsel so complained of pain and dizziness that Horn pulled the reins from his hands and gave the horse a savage slap. The animal started ahead at a good pace, though not quickly enough to satisfy Bolt, who continually turned back to urge more speed from the laboring nag. Even so, the company had gone less than a quarter mile when large raindrops pattered into the dust of the lane.

Arbican, huddled in a corner of the jolting wagon, had closed his eyes and bowed his head, withdrawn into himself.

"What's the matter with Hocus?" Wakeling asked. "He was lively enough when we found him."

"He's sick," answered Mallory. "If he stays here much longer, he may die."

"Nothing catching, is it?" Wakeling drew back uneasily.

"Please, please untie us," Mallory begged. "There's nobody watching, you won't be blamed for it."

Wakeling grinned. "That would be one in the eye for Squire, wouldn't it? And I can't say I'd mind seeing Bolt whistle for his money. Share the reward? If I get

so much as a penny in my pocket, that'll be a better trick than Old Hocus could pull off."

Wakeling seemed almost willing to do as Mallory asked. Just then, however, the wagon tilted so sharply that all three passengers went tumbling against the side, and Horn and Mr. Parsel nearly skidded off the seat. At Bolt's urging, Horn had recklessly ignored bumps and pot-holes; and this, added to all the other strains, had loosened one of the rear wheels, which now went spinning into a ditch.

Bolt reined up, cursing Mr. Parsel and his wagon alike. Wakeling scrambled down to retrieve the wheel, undamaged except for a couple of broken spokes. The angry gamekeeper ordered his prisoners to the side of the road and while Horn, Wakeling, and Mr. Parsel did their best to right the vehicle, Bolt unslung his musket and fired a shot in the air.

"Squire's hunting hereabouts," the gamekeeper said. "This should fetch him. He and I can ride double to the Holdings and get these two under lock and key."

"That's right, Bolt," retorted Horn. "Leave us to do the donkey work. The axle's bent. There's two good hours of labor in this muck, with dusk coming on. It's Parsel's cart; let him have the joy of mending it. I say march them across country, that's quickest."

Bolt thought for a moment, then nodded. "Unhitch Parsel's nag. You and I can both ride."

Hearing this, Mr. Parsel began bitterly protesting at being abandoned with a broken wagon as well as a broken head. Bolt turned to him:

"Pull it yourself, then. Or go to the devil, if that suits you better."

Neither suggestion pleased Mr. Parsel, who renewed his complaints all the louder, reproaching the gamekeeper for leaving a sick and prominent tradesman at the mercy of the elements, and vowing to report such behavior to the squire.

Hunched next to Arbican at the roadside, Mallory took no interest in the plans and counterplans for conducting her and the enchanter to the Holdings. While her captors turned their attention from their prisoners to their own disputes, she had not ceased to strain against the cords binding her wrists. At the same time, she weighed the risk of choosing an unguarded moment to spring up and dash for the woods. Arbican, she feared, would be too weak for that venture, and so she went back to tugging at her bonds, deciding that if she could break loose her only chance was to seize Bolt's musket. And that, she admitted to herself, would be far from easy.

In addition to the chafing of the cords, she grew aware of something uncomfortably jabbing into her side. The pocket of her dress had been empty; she could not remember putting anything in it. Puzzled, she cautiously twisted around until she was able to slip her hand into the pocket and draw out the contents. Even then, she could not bend enough to see what she had found; to her numb fingers, it felt smooth and flat.

"Arbican," she whispered, "can you tell what's in my hands?"

"Nothing I've seen in my day," replied the enchanter. "It looks made of tortoiseshell, apparently with a blade tucked into it. Hardly a formidable weapon, though it does seem to be a kind of folded-up knife."

"Of course it is! Mr. Parsel's! He always carries it, he pares his nails with it. It couldn't have dropped into my pocket by accident. He must have put it there." Astonished as much by Mr. Parsel's good deed as by finding the knife itself, she managed finally to unclasp the blade and cautiously began sawing away at the cords. However, her awkward posture and the need to work unnoticed made the task next to impossible. Although the rain had stopped, her bonds were wet, her fingers slippery; and Mr. Parsel, she realized, had gone to no pains to keep a sharp edge on his implement.

Try as she would, Mallory had barely cut through the first few strands when Bolt hastily mounted his horse and spurred to meet a pair of rapidly approaching riders. One, she saw with dismay, was Scrupnor on his bay mare, galloping in answer to the signal shot; but her spirits rose at sight of the other. It was Rowan.

Bolt soon joined his master and the notary; by the time the three reined up at the broken wagon, Mallory surmised that the gamekeeper had already given his own account of matters. Yet the squire's face was more grim than triumphant; and Rowan, as soon as he saw the two prisoners, jumped down from his horse and went straight to Mallory and Arbican.

"You'll answer for this, Bolt," the notary declared angrily. "Look at the state the old man is in; and the girl doesn't seem much better off."

"Stand away, Rowan," Scrupnor ordered, dismounting and hurrying after the notary. "They're both under arrest, by my authority as squire."

"I don't question your authority," answered Rowan. "But if you mean to use the law, you'll have to follow it yourself, as I've been telling you. Do you accuse this man of murder?"

"Accuse him?" cried Scrupnor. "I do more than that! I'll hang him!"

"Perhaps you will," replied the notary, "but only if you have evidence enough. Were stolen goods in his possession? Were there witnesses? Has he admitted his deed?"

"You're a bigger fool than I thought, notary," Scrupnor burst out. "As if this rogue would admit to anything! Do you think he'd carry the loot in his pockets? He's hidden it. Witnesses? My word's witness enough."

Rowan shook his head. "That won't do, Squire. Unless you have better proof, there's no true case against either of them. That's the law, Squire, and you'll set them free here and now."

CHAPTER
12

 Hearing this, Mallory started eagerly to her feet as Wakeling and Mr. Parsel stepped forward to carry out the notary's order. Scrupnor, however, put himself in their way:

"Not so fast, Rowan. There's no law going to quibble this scoundrel out of my hands. You'll see proof when the time comes."

"That may be, Squire," said Rowan. "Until then, you've no grounds for holding anyone."

"Haven't I?" answered Scrupnor. "If coldblooded murder isn't grounds enough to suit you, I'll give you another to serve in the meantime: common trespassing, and burglary on top of it. These two broke into my counting room. There's Bolt and all the household to stand witness. So, notary, go back to your law books."

"We didn't break in," Mallory protested angrily. "It wasn't that way at all—"

"You'll have a hearing," Rowan told her, making no attempt to hide his own distaste for Scrupnor's new accusation. "I can assure you of that much. For the rest—" He shook his head: "The squire's position is correct, if trespass is the charge he means to bring against you."

Mallory's heart sank as the notary turned away. Scrupnor, glowering, waited until Rowan had ridden out of sight, then curtly nodded to the gamekeeper:

"You've done well, Bolt." He glanced at Mallory and Arbican as if they were no more than a brace of trussed partridges.

"Let's have this pair up at the Holdings. You and I will take them. Let Horn and Wakeling see to the wagon."

As Bolt seemed about to disagree, Scrupnor cut him short:

"That's only fair, wouldn't you say, Bolt? You can't think of leaving one of our fine tradesmen stranded in the road, and badly injured into the bargain."

He climbed astride the bay and motioned for the gamekeeper to follow him with the prisoners. As he led the way across an open field toward a stretch of woodland, Mallory supposed he intended taking the shortest path to the Holdings. With Bolt walking his horse behind her, Mallory dared no further attempt at cutting her bonds. She was glad she had at least kept the knife instead of throwing it away during her moment of hope, and she held it hidden in her clenched palm, awaiting a chance to start the painful task again. Silent, Arbican trudged beside her.

Mallory had expected Scrupnor to be better satisfied by his victory over the notary, but his heavy jaw was clamped shut and his scowl had only deepened. Bolt, on the other hand, was in the best spirits; his face was flushed, his eyes glinted, and he seemed scarcely able to curb his impatience. While his master stayed moody, almost sullen, Bolt grew all the more talkative, telling again and again how, singlehanded, after fierce struggle, he had overcome the assassin:

"At risk of life and limb, Squire," he declared. "Mortal danger, nothing less. I'll not say anything against Horn and Wakeling, though one's a coward and the other a fool, and bunglers both. Well, forgive and forget; but if I was you, I'd send them packing. As for Parsel, he's sure to come snuffling and whimpering for a reward. As if he deserved it! The vixen could've run off any moment, and so she would have done if I hadn't come along when I did. But that's business between you and Parsel, and not my concern."

"Quite right," muttered Scrupnor. "Not your concern." The squire's tone showed little willingness to pursue the question. Bolt, however, cheerfully pressed on:

"In the matter of reward, Squire, as it just happened to pop into my head. Now, there was that thousand in gold you put up after old Sorrel got killed. But here's the fine point of it, Squire, and I wouldn't have you think I'm asking more than what's rightfully mine: But do you count that thousand apart and extra, or do you count it in with the Holdings?"

At this, the squire turned in the saddle to fix his eye on the gamekeeper:

"What the devil are you talking about?"

117

"Why, you know, Squire. At Parsel's table, Rowan himself was there, and you had him bear witness. You even wrote it all down and put your name to it, how you'd gladly give the Holdings to the fellow who caught Sorrel's murderer."

Scrupnor's face tightened, and he replied in a distant voice:

"Yes, Bolt, I might have done something like that."

"Might?" said the gamekeeper, frowning. "It's sure you did. I was in Parsel's kitchen and heard you with my own ears. And wouldn't the notary have that paper itself, all signed and sealed?"

"So I should think," Scrupnor nodded vaguely. "You forgot, Bolt, that I was the one who apprehended the felon."

"And lost him," said Bolt. "As you didn't keep him, in a manner of speaking you might say you, didn't truly catch him at all."

Scrupnor grimaced. "An intricate question. It will have to be studied out."

This answer seemed not altogether satisfying to Bolt, and Mallory had the impression the gamekeeper wished to continue the matter. Scrupnor, however, turned his mare and spurred the animal off the path. She saw he was heading for a small cottage whose plaster walls showed a spider web of cracks, and dark stains below the narrow windowsills.

"Hullo, there's my lodge," exclaimed Bolt. "With all this talk between men of affairs, and my mind on those intercut questions, as you call them, I could have passed it by and never noticed."

"We'll rest here, Bolt," said Scrupnor.

"Rest? Why, Squire, we're hardly a skip and a jump from the Holdings. Those two don't need a rest. If they lag, I can liven them up a bit."

"No doubt," said Scrupnor. "Even so, we'll stop a moment or two."

Disregarding Bolt's protest that his lodge was at the moment unprepared to receive such an honored guest, Scrupnor dismounted and beckoned for the gamekeeper to bring Mallory and Arbican inside.

The main room of the lodge was close and damp, with a rank odor that caught at Mallory's nostrils. A rumpled cot stood against one wall; by the fireplace hung string of gutted hares and pheasants, suggesting to her that Bolt was not unwilling to poach a little of the game he was charged to protect.

Scrupnor, however, chose to overlook the hares and pheasants. If Bolt appeared ill at ease and put out of face by his uninvited visitor, Mallory noticed the squire's mood had changed for the better as he glanced around the room and nodded his approval.

"Very snug," said Scrupnor in a cordial tone, "very nicely fitted out. Where can you store those two and keep them out of the way for a little while?"

Bolt shook his head. "Why, I don't know, Squire. We don't want Old Nick too far out of hand, do we? Nor the wench, slippery as she is." He pointed to a trap door near the fireplace. "There's the root cellar."

"Splendid," replied Scrupnor, motioning for the gamekeeper to lock up his charges immediately.

Bolt was none too gentle in bundling Mallory and Arbican down the few wooden steps. For Mallory, however, the root cellar could not have been more welcome. No sooner had Bolt dropped the trap door back in place than she began cutting at her bonds again. The dank earthen walls around her and the floodboards above her head gave no room to stand, and she could only crouch, making herself small as she could. Arbican was hunched in a corner, his legs cramped under his chin. The cellar, at least, was not entirely dark; some light came through the cracks in the planking and, by pressing her eye against them, she was able to catch glimpses of Scrupnor and Bolt near the hearth.

"Now, Bolt," she heard Scrupnor go on in a low, cajoling voice, "you know me as a man of my word. You've served me well in this business and I'll be open-handed with you. A thousand in gold? Not half enough, not for a fine fellow like you. No, double that. Two thousand, I say. Perhaps a bit more if all goes as it should. That's a fat purse, wouldn't you say? More than enough to satisfy any reasonable man. Think of it, Bolt. You could travel anywhere you please, set yourself up very handsomely someplace—"

"Why, Squire," broke in the gamekeeper, "I don't have a mind for travel, that's not my nature. A fat purse, as you say. But not so fat as the Holdings."

"Wait a minute, Bolt," said Scrupnor. "You go too fast. As you remind me, I did endorse a certain statement. But the circumstances must be taken into account. I made my offer in good faith, at that moment. A moment of pure grief. I was carried away in a paroxysm of turmoil. I'm softhearted, Bolt, as you well know. I'd have given all I owned in this world—and still would, if only it were possible. Alas, we cannot always follow the urgings of our hearts. We must, painful and incommodious as it may be, temper our desires with practicality." Scrupnor paused, sighed heavily, then quietly added:

"Tell me, Bolt, do you seriously think I'd give up the Holdings? To you or anyone else?"

Bolt grinned. "Of course you wouldn't, Squire. I know that. Don't take me for a fool. All those crocodile tears and signing and witnessing—a bit of play-acting, Squire, since you couldn't get out of it. No, you wouldn't give away all the Holdings. But I think you'll give me half, and be glad and grateful I don't take more. Now, there's that coal pit you mean to put down; and all the trade to come from that road of yours; and old Parsel's inn, and all the rest. That part of the business, we share and share alike. Partners, you and me."

Mallory pressed her eyes closer to the crack. Scrupnor, she saw, was looking narrowly at the gamekeeper. She felt the first of the cords begin to give way and she doubled her efforts as she heard the squire say:

"Come, come, Bolt. We're men of the world. Justice is beyond price, as I'm first to admit. But the cost of applying it, something else again. Partners? Share alike? No, Bolt, you can't expect me to half-beggar myself for the sake of hanging a common criminal."

"Oh, he's not a common criminal," Bolt answered. "He's no criminal at all."

"What?" cried Scrupnor. "That murderer—"

"Him?" The gamekeeper laughed. "Him, strangle a man? He doesn't have strength to squash a fly. He's not the one, you know that as well as I. Now, Squire, if it suits your purpose to say he killed Sorrel, I'll play your game along with you, to be friendly and obliging. As for the fellow who really killed the old gent—less said about him, the better, if you take my meaning. Justice? No. Where you get your money's worth is: silence."

"You're sharp, Bolt," Scrupnor said quietly after a moment. "Sharper than I thought. A gold mine of sharpness. A man could do worse than have you for his partner. Indeed, as I think of it, I wouldn't want it otherwise. I'll need to keep an eye on you, from now on."

"And the other way round, too, Squire."

"Quite right. We'll both look out for each other. That's twice as safe. Settled, then? Now that we have our little understanding?"

By this time, Mallory had cut through the last of the strands. She turned hastily and freed Arbican from his bonds. She put her eye to the crack again. Bolt, she saw, had come to stand near the trap door:

"We do understand each other, Squire, and that's a pleasure for two gentlemen to know each other's mind. As for Old Scratch, if Rowan must have his hearing all legal as it should be, he'll have to be there. That's only proper. But the less he says, the better. Best yet, he says nothing at all. In short, Squire, I doubt we'll want him there alive."

"My conclusion exactly," replied Scrupnor. "If Rowan wants proof he's a born murderer, he shall have it. It seems to me that Old Scratch, as you so nicely call him, would do well to try to escape; a fatal error in

122

judgment on his part. It would simplify matters. We should then be able to answer for him much better than he can answer for himself."

"The wench, too."

Scrupnor sighed. "Yes, that would be best for all concerned. As I don't know what she saw in the counting room, I think it safer for her to participate in a serious accident."

"What she saw?" said the gamekeeper. "Come, Squire, no secrets between us."

"Nothing to trouble you, Bolt," said Scrupnor. He rubbed his hands briskly. "Now, I'm afraid we have an unhappy task ahead of us. A cold business, at best. I should enjoy a fire. And a little drop of something."

Mallory stared, too terrified to move, as Bolt took a bottle and two chipped glasses from the cupboard. Setting them on the table, he indicated that Scrupnor should have the honor of pouring, then knelt at the hearth and began laying the fire. Scrupnor had picked up the bottle, but now put it down again and came to watch the gamekeeper.

"Excellent," said Scrupnor. "That will do nicely. Though it may need kindling there in the back. Spread it a little more. Here, let me show you."

Smiling blandly, Scrupnor took a poker from the stand of fire irons. As the gamekeeper busied himself with the kindling, Scrupnor, still smiling, raised the poker and with all his might brought it down on Bolt's head.

Mallory could not stifle her scream as she saw the gamekeeper pitch forward across the hearth. With a

thoughtful look, Scrupnor calmly struck once more, then stooped to peer at the body. Satisfied, he threw aside the poker and wiped his hands on Bolt's packet. Sick with horror, Mallory saw him return bottle and glasses to the cupboard, where he stood a moment, whistling softly through his teeth. His hand went to the pistol at his belt; then, thinking better of it, he replaced the weapon and again picked up the power. Mallory shrank back as he strode to the root cellar, bent, and flung open the door.

"Come out," Scrupnor ordered in a flat voice.

In the moment he took to realize Mallory's hands were free, she leaped up the steps, grappled Scrupnor around the legs, and sent him tumbling back. Flailing the poker, Scrupnor tried to fight her off, while Mallory shouted for Arbican to run from the lodge.

By force of weight and strength, Scrupnor tore himself loose from Mallory's hold. He gripped the poker in both hands and swung it downward. Helpless, Mallory could only shield her head with her arms. Behind, her, she heard Arbican's voice cry out words in a strange tongue.

The poker, that instant, flew from Scrupnor's grasp. It spun through the air and whirled in circles around him, belaboring him at every turn.

"Get out!" Arbican commanded Mallory. "Quick! The spell won't last."

Instead of obeying, Mallory seized the enchanter by the cloak and pulled him, protesting, through the door. Untethering Bolt's horse, she boosted Arbican into the saddle and ran to leap astride the mare.

No sooner had Arbican crossed the threshold than

125

the poker ceased its drubbing and fell clattering to the floor. Bruised and battered, roaring furiously, Scrupnor burst from the lodge, pistol in his hand.

Galloping for the woods, Mallory heard the shot ring out behind her. Arbican slumped forward in the saddle.

CHAPTER
13

 The enchanter clung to the horse's mane. Drawing alongside, Mallory caught the reins he had dropped and pulled both mounts to a halt.

"Blast those pistols or whatever you call them," Arbican muttered. "Despicable devices. In my day bows and arrows went far enough."

Mallory could hear Scrupnor crashing through the brush, bellowing in rage. Hastily examining Arbican's wound, she could only see that the bullet had struck him in the side and he was bleeding heavily. She sprang down from the mare and remounted behind the enchanter. Hoping Scrupnor would follow the wrong trail, or at least be misled for a time, she slapped the flanks of the bay and sent the animal plunging in a different direction.

She pressed on half-blindly in the gathering dusk, urging the already lathered horse to a faster gait.

Arbican sagged and grew heavier in her arms as she tried to keep him from toppling out of the saddle. For a while, he had been silent, not even grumbling; now he begged her to stop and rest. She halted, helped the enchanter to the ground, and sat him down in a pile of leaves, his back against a tree trunk.

This appeared to ease him. He gave a long sigh, opened his eyes, and murmured:

"I've been trying spells against sword wounds, spear thrusts, even snake bites. Nothing answers. At this point, I doubt I have power enough to heal myself of a bee sting. Well, no matter. I'll sleep for a while; that certainly, should be easy enough to do."

"We can't stay here," Mallory insisted, as the enchanter closed his eyes and turned his face aside. "We'll find our way to the village. You'll need bandages and medicine—"

"I'm quite aware of that," replied Arbican. "Are you able to conjure them up? I'm not. Besides, my time is running out; I can sense that. So, this is as good a place as any."

"What are you saying?" Mallory cried. "You're just going to give up? Sit here and do nothing? For an enchanter, that's not very brave."

"But very sensible," said Arbican. "It's apparent to me, as it should be to you, there's no possible way of building a boat, let alone finding a circle of gold. As for the village, I've no desire to go hacking and stumbling through these woods. No, I prefer some last dignity and self-respect."

"Rowan would help us," Mallory urged, "if he knew what Scrupnor did. And there's Emmet, the harnessmaker, he's always been good to me. Mr. Parsel means well, he did give me his knife; but I daren't go to the cook-shop, not with Mrs. Parsel around."

"As I just finished explaining, I prefer—"

"Listen to me," Mallory pressed on. "When we went to the Holdings—couldn't you do the same, and take us to Rowan's house?"

Arbican shook his head. "I doubt it. After that business with the poker, I'm afraid I've come to the end of my strength."

"You can try, can't you?" Mallory urged. "In all the tales, when everything's at worst, that's when the hero tries his best."

"Unadulterated fiction," retorted Arbican. "In my time, it was a mark of common sense to know a hopeless situation when you saw one. It's only in those fabricated accounts you mortals have invented—"

"Invented?" Mallory flung back. "I don't care! If that's how things were in your day, I like my fairy tales better!"

Arbican blinked indignantly, opened his mouth to reply, then snapped it shut, and fell silent and brooding. After a long moment, he fixed his eyes on Mallory:

"Very well. Give me your hand. You must guide me, as you did before."

Mallory closed her eyes and tried to picture in her mind the house of the notary, only to realize in alarm that of all places in the village this was one she knew least. Her vision of it broke apart and faded. Exhausted, she fought to summon it back again, now hardly able even to recall the narrow winding street near the cook-shop. Arbican, meantime, had begun murmuring to

himself. In another moment, the ground dropped away beneath her feet. Wrenched and buffeted, she felt her hand slip from the enchanter's grasp.

Light flared in her eyes as a candle was thrust at her face. A white-robed figure loomed before her, and a noise like a knife on a grindstone rasped in her ears. Wrapped in a trailing night robe, hair bristling with curlpapers, it was Mrs. Parsel.

Arbican lay on the kitchen floor. While Mrs. Parsel yelled furiously for her husband, Mallory stumbled to the enchanter's side. Arbican was unconscious, but still alive. Seeing the enchanter, Mrs. Parsel shrieked all the louder, "It's him! The murderer! Come to strangle us all! Parsel, defend your wife! Get the meat ax!"

At the same time, Mrs. Parsel set down the candle and snatched a broom from the corner, ready to defend life and limb. In answer to his wife's urgent command, Mr. Parsel slowly and cautiously peered around the kitchen door. Nightcap askew on his bandaged head, his face pale and puffy, he looked scarcely recovered from his ordeal in the road. He gasped in disbelief at Mallory and Arbican; however, instead of seeking the weapon Mrs. Parsel demanded, he sat down heavily on a chair, opened and shut his eyes rapidly, as though trying to rouse himself from a discomforting dream.

"Help him," pleaded Mallory, hurrying to Mr. Parsel. "Scrupnor shot him. He may be dying."

Mr. Parsel clapped his hands to his head. "Oh dear, oh dear, you should never have brought him to the house. You should never have come back. Shot? Dying? Good heavens, he mustn't do it here!"

At last sure that Arbican was not about to leap up

and strangle her, Mrs. Parsel triumphantly waved her broom:

"I've got him, that foul assassin! Murder will out! Justice will be served! Parsel, our fortune's made!"

"Tell her," Mallory urged. "Arbican's done nothing. You believe that. You must, or you wouldn't have given me your knife."

Hearing this, Mrs. Parsel, with a horrified gasp, turned on her husband. "You did what? You gave what?"

"Please, listen to me," Mallory broke in. "If Mr. Parsel hadn't helped us, we'd both be dead now—"

"Parsel, you fool," cried Mrs. Parsel in a terrible voice, "what have you done?"

"My dear, don't work yourself up," begged Mr. Parsel. "You know your delicate constitution; you can't stand such excitement."

"Parsel, am I to understand you aided and abetted?"

"I wasn't thinking clearly," protested Mr. Parsel. "A rash moment—I lost my head, I don't know what came over me."

"Lost your head?" roared Mrs. Parsel. "That's no loss at all! You could have lost your hypothecation!"

While Mr. Parsel stammered apologies for his good deed, and while Mrs. Parsel kept on with her tongue lashing, Mallory tried to tend Arbican's wound. The bleeding had stopped and she saw that Scrupnor's bullet had caused less damage than she had supposed. More serious, she feared, was the enchanter's exhaustion. However, as she was about to search the cook-shop for medicine, spirits, or whatever might serve to revive

Arbican, Mrs. Parsel barred her way with the broomstick.

"And you, ungrateful wretch! After all my care and kindness! Do you know how much that old rogue's worth? Were you trying to get all the reward for yourself?"

"There's no reward," Mallory flung back. "Scrupnor's lied to you. He killed Bolt. And he killed Squire Sorrel, too."

"Bite your tongue!" Mrs. Parsel cried. "How dare you say that? There's no more generous, thoughtful—"

"Except for my hypothecation," put in Mr. Parsel, who had been sitting hunched into himself, ready at any moment to shield his head against his wife's broom. "That's sharp practice, no other word for it."

"And you, hold your tongue!" ordered Mrs. Parsel. "That's your own fault for being such a fool."

"Don't you understand what I'm telling you?" Mallory cried. "Bolt's dead! Scrupnor split his head with a poker. I was there. I saw it. Arbican isn't to blame for anything. He's an enchanter. I found him in a tree."

"It's happened at last," declared Mrs. Parsel to her husband. "I told you it would and now it has. The girl's gone mad. The fairy tales have burst her brain."

Mallory held back no longer. In a last attempt to convince Mrs. Parsel, she poured out the whole account of Arbican's mishaps. When she finished, Mrs. Parsel said nothing, and only shook her head.

Mr. Parsel, to Mallory's relief, seemed greatly cheered and reassured. "There, you see, my dear, I did the right thing after all. A wizard, indeed! Whoever would have thought it! I daresay he'll have some tales to tell us. Does he read tea leaves? Perhaps he'll give me some advice about my hypothecation? Now, let's see what we can do for him."

"We shall do what our duty requires," said Mrs. Parsel. "But look at the state of this poor girl! Calm yourself, child. After what you've gone through, no wonder you're feverish. I'll give you a bowl of hot milk."

"Arbican needs care more than I do," Mallory said.

"He shall have it," replied Mrs. Parsel, ordering her husband to fetch whatever was needed while she herself went to rummage in the pantry. By the time the promised milk was ready, Arbican had regained his senses and was able to sit up. Mallory helped him swallow a few mouthfuls from the steaming basin, and gratefully drank some herself.

For the first time she was able to breathe easily. After the chill of the woods, she now felt pleasantly warm, as if she were sitting by a comfortable fire. Arbican was dozing peacefully and soon Mallory began to yawn, and her eyelids drooped.

"We'd better get word to Rowan," Mallory murmured. "Arbican will need a safe place to sleep, in the meantime. No telling what Scrupnor may try to do."

"We'll make up a lovely feather bed for your friend, my dear," said Mrs. Parsel. "Don't worry about a thing. He'll have a nice nap. And so will you. After that sleeping draught, you'll be in dreamland for some while."

Mallory's lips had turned numb and her cry of

134

horror came as little more than a slurred whisper. Mrs. Parsel had drawn closer, watching Mallory intently. The curlpapers seemed to turn her head into a huge dandelion puff that floated before Mallory's eyes, hung a few moments in the air, then drifted away altogether.

 Mallory struggled to open her eyes. At first, she remembered there had been muffled sounds in darkness, the distant voice of Mrs. Parsel, the neighing of a horse. Now rough hands were setting her on her feet. Helpless, she went stumbling, half-carried down a hallway, and through a door. She vaguely recognized Scrupnor's counting room. Arbican, still fast asleep, stretched beside her in a corner near the shelves of papers and account books.

"Mrs. Parsel," Mallory heard Scrupnor say, "you're a woman of resolution and determination, to bring me these malefactors singlehanded."

"Squire, I had no choice," replied Mrs. Parsel. "There was no use to be had from Parsel. He's been ailing and addled ever since that blow to his head. But you,

Squire, if you allow me a personable observation, you yourself appear to have suffered a mischance."

"That, Mrs. P., is to say the very least of it," returned Scrupnor, passing a hand over his bruised face. "You see before you the unsuspecting victim of assault and battery." He paused a moment, then added in a grave tone: "With intent to kill."

At this, Mallory tried to protest; but the sleeping potion still gripped her and she could barely raise her head. Mrs. Parsel, however, gasped as though the squire's life were still in danger. Scrupnor raised a reassuring hand:

"Be calm, Mrs. P. My wounds are superfluous. They are nothing compared with the two I carry here." Scrupnor pointed to the upper portion of his waistcoat.

"What, Squire," cried Mrs. Parsel, "were you stabbed, as well?"

"Deeply, Mrs. P., deeply. In the figurative sense, but no less painful for all that. I refer not only to the demise of my benefactor but, only a few short hours ago, to the brutal slaying of one who was more than a faithful servant. Mr. Bolt is no longer with us. He succumbed to a poker. A humble domestic utensil turned into a weapon of murder." At this, Scrupnor pointed a finger at Arbican. "Wielded ruthlessly, relentlessly, by the selfsame criminal who snatched away the life and breath of Squire Sorrel.

"I defended the unfortunate Mr. Bolt as best I could," Scrupnor went on. "Don't let his gray hairs deceive you, that bearded villain has the strength of a dozen devils. You see his handiwork engraved on my brow. Alas, I could not save Mr. Bolt's life. Indeed, I might have lost my own if I had not succeeded in putting that hardened criminal to flight."

"The truth at last!" exclaimed Mrs. Parsel. "Oh, Squire, what a relief and pleasure to hear the facts, grievous as they are. And this—this depraved, vicious, treacherous creature I raised by hand, with every comfort and cosset, dared to say that you were the one who struck down poor Mr. Bolt."

Scrupnor's jaw dropped. For a speechless moment he stared at Mallory, then shook his head. "Did she say that, Mrs. P.? Poor deranged child. What a curious fancy. A remarkable imagination—but, alas, an unwholesome one."

"It's the fairy tales," Mrs. Parsel said. "They've chewed away at her mind until there's hardly a rind left. Squire, if you had heard what else she babbled about: wizards coming out of trees, turning into pigs—"

Scrupnor clicked his tongue. "What a burden you've borne, Mrs. P. But you shall bear it no longer. The matter is now in my hands. Leave her with me. She shall be looked after. Be proud you have done your duty; that knowledge will ease the pain of your loss."

Scrupnor bowed and gestured toward the counting room door. Mrs. Parsel, however, made no move to rise from her chair.

"But, Squire," she said, "you'll surely want to wait for Mr. Rowan. I sent Parsel to fetch him. Drat the man, he's so slow and bumbling, and all the worse since his accident. But they'll be along directly."

Scrupnor's smile wavered an instant. "Fetch Mr. Rowan? Why should you have done a thing like that?"

"For your convenience," replied Mrs. Parsel, "thinking you'd want to settle the reward here and now, and get all such details out of the way. It's never wise to delay matters of business, as you yourself know."

"I'm sorry you did that, Mrs. P.," said Scrupnor, his smile crumbling entirely. "It was labor lost. For I shall now be obliged to tell them you aren't here."

Mrs. Parsel frowned a little. "Why, Squire, why ever should you say a thing like that?"

"In fact," Scrupnor went on thoughtfully, as much to himself as to Mrs. Parsel, "it would be simpler to tell them you never arrived here in the first place."

Mallory's arms and legs still weighed more than she could lift. Her tongue felt thick and she could scarcely form her words as she murmured:

"I told you. What he did to Bolt. Now, you too."

"She's raving again," said Mrs. Parsel, although with a certain uneasiness. She stood up hastily. "You don't think for a moment I believe a word of what she said. Indeed, I hardly listened. Who would pay attention to such delirious accusations? Not I, Squire, that I swear to you."

When Scrupnor did not answer, Mrs. Parsel hurried on:

"Ah, yes, it would be better to save our business for a happier moment. These distressful events have put a strain on all of us. I can see you're not quite yourself. A good night's sleep will work wonders. Tomorrow, I'll bring you a pot of my calves'-foot jelly, that has always been very curative."

Mrs. Parsel would have made her way to the door, but Scrupnor stepped in front of her. "That's thoughtful of you, Mrs. P., but unnecessary. Calves'-foot jelly? Ah, if only our cares and concerns could be lightened with a little calves'-foot jelly, the world would be a happier place."

"Mr. Scrupnor," declared Mrs. Parsel, trying to hide her growing alarm with indignation, "allow me to depart for my residence."

"If only that were possible," Scrupnor answered regretfully, barring the door with an upraised arm. "But you must appreciate the difficulties of my position. Loose talk, gossip, idle chatter—these have a way of leading to embarrassing questions. Far better to eliminate the source altogether, to nip them in the bud—"

"I won't breathe a word!" cried Mrs. Parsel. "My lips are sealed!"

"I'm sure they will be," replied Scrupnor. "In this world so full of uncertainty, at least that is absolutely beyond a doubt."

"What of Parsel?" exclaimed Mrs. Parsel. "He's heard the girl's story as much as I have—I mean, he paid no more attention than I did. What of Rowan?"

"Our honest notary, as I have reason to know, puts great store in evidence. Since there is none—or will be none—I don't see much he can do about it. As for Mr. Parsel, I doubt he would be so foolish, as you and the late Mr. Bolt have been, to concern himself with money I have no intention of paying. Indeed, I may very well have to assure myself of Mr. Parsel's silence, too. We shall see. But first, we must deal with problems immediately to hand; of which, at the moment, there happen to be three in my counting room.

140

"It would be best, I think," Scrupnor continued, "if all of you unfortunately had met with a fatal accident on your way to the Holdings. As I see it, the old man woke up and attacked you both—a concealed weapon might be in order, possibly a butcher knife. Then, with appalling lack of caution, got himself run over by the wagon. Certain small refinements may occur to me in progress, but the outcome will be the same. Meantime, I shall go and be surprised by the arrival of your husband and the notary. Forgive me, Mrs. P., but the circumstances are as painful to me as they are to you. However, in this difficult world, we must all bow to necessity."

With a shriek, Mrs. Parsel threw herself upon the squire. Despite her bulk, she was no match for him and he heaved her back into the counting room. Mallory, with great effort, had climbed unsteadily to her feet, too late to help Mrs. Parsel or to keep Scrupnor from stepping hastily out of the door and locking it behind him.

Arbican, too, had awakened and was struggling to rise. Seeing the enchanter stumbling toward her, and convinced he meant to take some ghastly revenge for what she had done, Mrs. Parsel rolled up her eyes and fainted dead away.

Mallory turned from her useless battering of the door and looked around for anything to serve as tool or weapon; but there was not even a stand of fire irons by the empty hearth.

"Arbican, have you power for one more spell? Anything, no matter, just to get us out of here."

141

Arbican grimaced. "At this point, I haven't magic enough to boil a pot of water. It's gone for sure; our last venture was the end of it."

"Did you hear Scrupnor? He's going to make it look as if you killed us. He must have done as much with Squire Sorrel. He always claimed he went to Castleton, but I'm sure he didn't. He must have come back during the night and broken into the Holdings himself—"

"A fascinating speculation," Arbican replied. "True, no doubt, but no help to us now. I see only one thing: We shall have to take him by surprise when he comes back."

"He's stronger than both of us together. Oh, blast Mrs. Parsel and her sleeping draught. My head's still going round. Fight him? He'll have his pistol."

"That damnable thing? Yes, I suppose he will," said the enchanter. "Very well, we shall have to hit him with something. The chair? Break it up and use the legs for clubs? Crude, but not ineffective."

"That might do," Mallory agreed. "Or—something heavier? One of the stones from the fireplace. They seem loose enough to pull out. Wait—could we climb up the chimney?"

"Too risky," Arbican warned. "If we got stuck in it, he'd have us neatly trapped. Furthermore, I'm hardly in condition to go squirming through layers of soot."

Mallory, nevertheless, had gone to peer into the fireplace. Soot would be the least of their worries. The hearth, she saw, was swept clean and the fireplace seemed quite unused. "The chimney's wide enough," she called. "For us, at least. But no way in the world for

142

Mrs. Parsel. Besides, there's a stone blocking the flue. I'll try to pull it out."

The task demanded less effort than she had imagined, for the stone came free almost immediately. Thrusting her head and shoulders into the opening, Mallory cried out in surprise. On a narrow ledge lay a tin cashbox.

"Arbican—look, Scrupnor's hidden something in the chimney."

"I'm not interested in what he's squirreled away. Let it be. Come, help me move this table. We shall first barricade the door."

Mallory, however, had already begun to pry open the container. She gasped as a gold watch, a jeweled snuffbox, gold chains and lockets spilled into her hands.

"These are Squire Sorrel's!" Mallory exclaimed. "Here's his crest engraved—"

The door just then was thrown open and Scrupnor strode across the threshold. For an instant he hesitated at the sight of Mallory holding the box; but his scowl vanished as he nodded with satisfaction.

"I see you've found my little keepsakes. So much the better. You've given me a most excellent idea; one, I admit, which had not occurred to me."

"You did kill Squire Sorrel," cried Mallory. "You made it look as if he'd been robbed. Here's the proof of it!"

"Proof beyond question," Scrupnor admitted cheerfully. "Evidence incontrovertible. All the more convincing when found in the murderer's possession, as it will be, I assure you. And you've also helped me with another small difficulty.

"I always admired those trinkets," continued

Scrupnor. "I tell you very frankly it pained me, having to hide them away. They're such charming objects—and highly valuable, in addition, of course, to their being fond remembrances of the late lamented. You saw that for yourself, the day you and your accomplice came bursting in here."

"Is that what you thought?" returned Mallory. "I saw nothing at all! I wish I had, for I'd have gone straight to Rowan and told him."

"Of course you would," agreed Scrupnor. "But that danger is past, it makes no difference now. Once these items are discovered on the criminal cadaver, I shall claim them rightfully as part of the estate. It will be a source of profoundest satisfaction to wear the late lamented's watch and his signet ring. In regard to which: Give them here."

But Mallory, drawing closer to the enchanter, was staring at the heavy gold ring. "Arbican—will this help you?" she cried. "It's gold! It's a circle! Here, I give it to you!"

Before the enchanter could reply, Mallory pressed the ring into his hand. With a growl of impatience, Scrupnor, hand outstretched, started toward Arbican. That instant, however, the enchanter's bent shoulders straightened and his eye suddenly blazed.

"No closer!" he commanded. "Beware! My power's at full flood! Touch me not!"

Arbican's face glowed; the air shimmered and crackled around him. Both wonder-struck and frightened at this new sight of the enchanter, Mallory flung up her arms to shield her eyes. Scrupnor, however, had

already sprung forward and locked his hands around Arbican's thoat.

A clap of thunder burst in Mallory's ears, and the shock of it threw her to the ground. Her last glimpse was of Arbican, arms raised and outspread, the flaming branches of a tree.

CHAPTER
15

 Arbican had vanished. Mallory, stunned and shaken, staggered to her feet and called out his name. There was no trace of him. Only the gold ring lay where he had stood. Scrupnor, too, was gone; one of his boots and a charred waistcoat smouldered near the fireplace. Mrs. Parsel, coming to her senses, heaved herself up and blinked around her.

"Where is he?" she demanded angrily, once she was certain Scrupnor was no longer in the room. "Where is that villainous creature? That hypocrite! That molester of a helpless woman? Let me face him!"

Too alarmed over Arbican's disappearance to answer Mrs. Parsel, Mallory had begun searching every corner. At the same time, there came a violent battering at the door; in another moment, it burst from its hinges and Mr. Parsel tumbled through, with the notary at his heels.

Seeing his wife safe and her temper as undamaged as the rest of her, Mr. Parsel threw his arms around Mallory, who could not hold back her sobs as she tried to recount what had happened.

"Now, now, Mallie," Mr. Parsel soothed, "your friend's bound to turn up again. People don't go disappearing into thin air, least of all elderly gentlemen—"

"He's an enchanter," insisted Mallory. "Do you still not believe me? I have to find him. I don't know if he's even alive. Come with me, help me look."

"I should advise against that," put in Rowan, who had been examining the contents of the cashbox. He glanced at the empty boot. "From what's left here, I doubt you will find him or the squire, either. I doubt you would really want to. It would, I fear, be painful for you."

"Well, it won't be painful for me," declared Mrs. Parsel. "If I ever lay hands on—on that individual! Threatening me as he did! To think I offered him calves'-foot jelly! To think I invited him to the Ladies' Benevolence!"

"I suggest, ma'am, you let matters rest as they are," said Rowan. "There has been very strange business here tonight. I, for one, mean to confine myself to the facts as I see them and urge you to do the same. Squire Scrupnor is gone. Should he ever be found alive, he will surely go to trial, and just as surely hang. The evidence speaks for itself. That, for me, is quite sufficient. Beyond that, the rest can be only wild speculation."

"Be glad it turned out as it did," Mr. Parsel said. "I should hate to think what would have happened if Mr.

Rowan and I hadn't seen the wagon in the yard, after Squire telling us you weren't here."

"If you hadn't been so slow about it," returned Mrs. Parsel, "you'd have spared your wife the humiliation and indignity of being put upon by that loathsome wretch. That creature has been a disappointment to me. A disappointment, nothing less."

"My dear," said Mr. Parsel, "if you'd listened to Mallie in the first place—"

While Mrs. Parsel continued to upbraid her husband, Mallory turned away and put her head in her hands, trying to make herself believe, in spite of what she had seen, that Arbican was still alive. Her hope, nevertheless, was not enough to overcome her grief. Nothing, she told herself bitterly, happened as it should. The fairy tales she loved now seemed to mock her, and she understood a little why Arbican so belittled them. Even magic itself had betrayed her. The circle of gold she had given him, the spell that should have saved him, had only destroyed him.

Mr. Parsel put a hand on her shoulder. "Come along, Mallie. We'll go home now."

Mrs. Parsel, however, had turned her attention from her husband to the notary. "It has been a trying, disconcerting day, Mr. Rowan, and one we should happily forget. But we should rest more comfortably in our beds if we might settle the obligations of—that despicable person."

The notary gave Mrs. Parsel a questioning look as she went on:

"Certain financial inducements had been offered, in the nature, you might say, of a reward. Indeed, Mr.

Rowan, as you very well know, it includes possession of the Holdings themselves."

"I do know that," answered the notary. "And whether Mr. Scrupnor is alive or dead, his offer is still binding. However, the best claim to the property lies with the person who last, and most directly apprehended the murderer. Namely, Mr. Arbican."

"What are you saying?" cried Mrs. Parsel, turning more pale at the prospect of losing the reward than she had done at the prospect of losing her life. "That we're to have nothing for our pains? Arbican? We don't know who he is, where he came from, or where he's gone. But gone he is, and that leaves Parsel and me."

"No, it does not!" cried Mr. Parsel, before the notary could answer. "No, Mrs. P., it most certainly does not!"

Mrs. Parsel stared at her husband, who had drawn himself up to his full height, and whose pudgy cheeks were quivering like those of an infuriated rabbit.

"Parsel!" she cried. "Hold your tongue!"

"Mrs. Parsel," returned the cook-shop owner, "I will not! You egged me on to get myself hypothecated. You put it into my head to cheat on the victualization. I don't reproach you, Mrs. P., for I confess I wasn't unwilling. But there's the end of it. I should have spoken up before this, but I'll speak now. If anyone has a fair claim, it's Mallie."

"Exactly what I was about to say, Mr. Parsel," declared the notary. "I quite agree that in the absence of Mr. Arbican she has a very sound claim. Naturally, she will have to submit a formal statement, in writing. I shall draw up the paper."

At the double shock of being contradicted by her

husband and overreached by her servant, Mrs. Parsel choked, gasped, and seemed to have altogether lost her power of speech.

As for Mallory, it was a moment before she fully understood the notary's words. Then she turned to him. "No. I don't want the Holdings. I claim nothing at all."

CHAPTER
16

 It was daylight by the time Mallory rode from the Holdings. She hoped the men from the sawmill had not already hauled the oak away. "It's my tree, after all," she told herself, then corrected: "No, it's Arbican's. It always will be." At the clearing, she swung down from the bay mare and looked around in dismay. She had come too late. The oak was gone. Only the stump and a few broken twigs showed it had ever been there in the first place. After a moment, she turned sadly to remount. Then she cried out. Arbican was standing in front of her.

The wizard's cloak was as threadbare as ever, his beard as gray and straggling; but his bearing had changed, his eyes were sharp and commanding, and his gaze held her like a hand. For an instant, to her own astonishment, she was half afraid. Then, with a sob of relief, she ran to him:

"I was so sure you were dead—"

"An assumption obviously incorrect," Arbican replied. "In fact, my powers are stronger than ever. Perhaps a little too strong. Those years in the tree must have ripened them. Even I was surprised. They did get rather out of hand. I hardly expected to go blasting into thin air and end up here. I can tell you I had a few bad moments before I came to myself again. I was afraid I might have to pass the next few centuries disembodied, and you can imagine how irritating that would have been. But I have the knack of things again. As for that fellow Scrupnor—I'm sorry. It was his own fault. I warned him not to touch me. Aside from that, all's well."

"No—no, it isn't," Mallory began. "Arbican, something has happened—"

"Nothing serious, I'm sure," replied the wizard. "It could hardly be worse than what we've had to put up with."

"It is," Mallory said. "It's the Holdings. They're to be mine. All of them."

"In that case," answered Arbican, "congratulations. They couldn't be in better hands."

"You don't understand," Mallory insisted. "I didn't want them. I still don't want them. It was Mr. Parsel and Rowan who talked and badgered and finally I said I would, just to make them be quiet. But now—"

"It seems to me," Arbican broke in, "that you told me how you wished to be mistress of the manor."

"Yes, but that—that was only wishing."

"What, then," the enchanter sharply replied, "are you afraid to have your wishes come true?"

"I'm a kitchen maid," Mallory burst out. "I've been one all my life. How shall I deal with accounts, and tenants, and I don't know what all? I'll never make sense of running an estate."

"You'll make as much sense of it as anyone," Arbican said. "More than most, I should think."

"Rowan says you have the best claim to the Holdings," suggested Mallory.

But Arbican hastily shook his head.

"Out of the question. Wish all you want for yourself, but don't wish something like that on me."

"I've decided one thing," Mallory said. "If I have to be mistress of the manor, I'm going to let Mr. Parsel out of his hypothecation. He'll have his inn free and clear, and do what he likes with it. I've made up my mind about something else, too. I certainly won't pull down cottages for the sake of a coal mine. And Scrupnor's road—the damage is done, but I'll try to mend it somehow."

"So I hope," said Arbican, "though it may not be easy. Once things get started, you can't always stop them, much as you might like. Times change, you can't go back. No more than you can live in my world; no more than I can live in yours. The best you can do is use your common sense. Even then, things can turn out differently from what you wanted."

Mallory nodded. "Yes, you're right. Nothing ends as it does in fairy tales. I did love them so, and I did believe them. I'm sorry they aren't true."

"Not true?" cried Arbican. "Of course they're true! As true as you'll ever find."

"But you told me—"

"I never said such a thing! How could you have misunderstood me? Those tales of yours—yes, you people made them up. They aren't tales about *us*, though you may pretend they are. They're tales about yourselves, or at least the best parts of yourselves. They're not true in the outside world, mine or any other. But in the inside, yes, indeed. Now, come along with me."

Mallory followed the enchanter through the brush and down a slope to the riverbank. There he halted. At the water's edge bobbed a small boat of wood so polished that it seemed to flame. The lines of the hull swept forward like the curve of a harp. From the slender mast hung a sail golden in the sunlight. Despite the beauty of the vessel, Mallory felt her heart might break and she turned her eyes away.

"Good, eh?" said Arbican. "It took some doing, even for me. I've been busy at it since my abrupt departure from the counting room; that's why I didn't come back for you. I thought you might enjoy the surprise. You don't suppose I'd have gone without saying farewell?

"It's a neat, seaworthy craft," Arbican went on. "My oak tree had precisely the amount of wood I needed. The sail was a little afterthought of my own. Not really necessary; more ornamental than functional; but it does add a certain flair—"

He stopped. Mallory had said nothing, but the enchanter had understood her look, and he regretfully shook his head:

"No, child, it isn't possible. It never was. I told you that from the first. You have your own voyage to make, as I have mine."

"I know that," Mallory said, after a moment. "It's just that I couldn't help wishing—"

"So you must, always," Arbican quietly answered. "If your wish is strong enough, you may end up actually doing something to make it come true. I promised you a gift," he went on, "and I've been racking my brain for some little keepsake. I can think of nothing really suitable, so you shall have to suggest one. Within reason, of course."

"I want none," said Mallory. "Not any more. I shall remember you. Let that be gift enough."

"As I shall remember you," answered Arbican. "So be it. There's nothing of true value I could give that you don't have already."

"Farewell, then," Mallory said quietly, taking Arbican's hand in both her own.

The enchanter nodded. "Farewell." He touched his lips to her brow, turned away, and without a backward glance climbed aboard the boat which obediently floated clear of the bank, bearing toward the middle of the river.

The current caught the shining vessel, drawing it rapidly downstream. The wind freshened, billowing the golden sail; and the boat surged ahead impatiently. Mallory watched as the hunched figure in the stern grew smaller and smaller until it was out of sight.

MS READ-a-thon— a simple way to start youngsters reading

Boys and girls between 6 and 14 can join the MS READ-a-thon and help find a cure for Multiple Sclerosis by reading books. And they get two rewards — the enjoyment of reading, and the great feeling that comes from helping others.

Parents and educators: For complete information call your local MS chapter. Or mail the coupon below.

Kids can help, too!

- -

Mail to:
National Multiple Sclerosis Society
205 East 42nd Street
New York, N.Y. 10017

I would like more information about the MS READ-a-thon and how it can work in my area.

MS Mystery Sleuth™

Name _____
(please print)

Address _____

City _____ State _____ Zip _____

Organization _____

1—80